Cape Cod Stories

Tales from Cape Cod, Nantucket, and
Martha's Vineyard

EDITED BY JOHN MILLER AND TIM SMITH

D0974211

CHRONICLE BOOKS
SAN FRANCISCO

Library of Congress Cataloging-in-Publication-Data:

Cape Cod stories: tales from Cape Cod, Nantucket, and Martha's Vineyard / edited by John Miller and Tim Smith.
p.   cm.
ISBN 0-8118-1080-1
1. Short stories, American—Massachusetts. 2. Cape Cod (Mass.)—Social life and customs—Fiction. 3. Nantucket Island (Mass.)—Social life and customs—Fiction. 4. Martha's Vineyard (Mass.)—Social life and customs—Fiction. I. Miller, John, 1959-   .
II. Smith, Tim, 1962-   .
PS548.M4C37 1996
813'.01083274492—dc 20   95-42580
                                               CIP

Book and Cover design: Big Fish Books
Composition: Jennifer Petersen, Big Fish Books
Cover photograph: Joel Meyerowitz

Distributed in Canada by Raincoast Books
8680 Cambie Street, Vancouver B.C. V6P 6M9

10 9 8 7 6 5 4 3 2 1

Chronicle Books
275 Fifth Street
San Francisco, CA 94103

SPECIAL THANKS TO KIRSTEN MILLER

JOEL MEYEROWITZ

SUSAN GOLDBERG

SHELLEY BERNIKER

AND MARCIA BERNIKER

CONTENTS

Alice Hoffman

....

Introduction

OUT HERE, WE are always steps from the sea. Turn a corner in Hyannisport and it's just beyond the taffy shop. Walk through the pine woods in Truro, past the hollows where you can spy fox and deer at twilight, and it's there as well. Go to the very edge of the world, to Provincetown, and it will stretch out before you in a swell of sapphire or deep green, so unknowable and huge you'll want to drop to your knees and kiss the comfort of the earth.

We are a world of sea lavender and sea monsters, of hurricanes and skies as blue as heaven. When we talk, we talk

---

Alice Hoffman is the author of ten novels, including her latest,
Practical Magic. *She and her husband live near Boston.*

of tides. We speak of sharks and eels, of lobsters and oysters and whelks. And even when we have green lawns, and potted hydrangeas, and weeping willows and games of croquet, we know that just down the road, around the corner, past the general store, removed from the safety of our own small lives which are so filled with ordinary worries and ordinary cares, there is the sea. There is something to remind us that every minute is a mystery: What is smooth as glass can shatter and storm the minute you turn your back, it may pound at your boat, your heart, your house. What is wild and danger-ous can take you into its arms with calm seas and com-plete forgiveness.

I first came to the Cape in winter, to Province-town, with a foot of new snow falling on Route 6 and a frozen turkey in the back of my car. It was Christmas, and the town seemed empty of human life. Sea gulls hud-dled on the wharfs, their feathers shimmering with ice; the dunes were swept with snow. It seemed a place like no other on earth, a landscape where even the most ordi-nary thing—a cloud, a bird, the shift from daylight to night—was spectacular. That holiday I stayed with a friend, whom I later married, and my brother and sister-in-law, in a motel so close to the shore that at high tide the Atlantic Ocean rushed beneath our rooms. In this deserted town, so far out to sea, the salt on your skin, the tears in your eyes, makes you one with the landscape.

This intense connection with nature is what Melville speaks to when he writes of what makes a sailor from Nantucket so different from the rest—why such a man owns the sea "as the Emperors own empires."

> With the landless gull, that at sunset folds her wings and is rocked to sleep between billows; so at nightfall, the Nantucketer, out of sight of land, furls his sails, and lays him to rest, while under his very pillow rush herds of walruses and whales.

Those dreams of walruses and whales, of emperors and of sails, have brought writers to the Cape year after year. Most come in June, when the fireflies first appear, and leave (back to solid land, to the universities where they teach and the cities where they make their winter homes) by September, when there are still tomatoes growing on the vine. Some are lucky enough to live here all year round, and, as Louise Rafkin's "Provincetown Diary" shows us, the Cape is cheap (off season) and beautiful (all seasons). As a year-round resident you can know all your neighbors and everyone who works in the post office and still find solitude. We are all grateful to our patron saint, the late Speaker of the House, Tip O'Neill, for that. Years ago, he was hung in effigy in the town hall at Wellfleet by business owners and fishermen who were convinced O'Neill was standing in the way of progress. Now, we bless him for the National Seashore, which he helped to establish in 1961. We still have our wild lands, our moors and dunes and pine woods; we can still hear the owls take flight.

But Cape Cod is also Hyannisport, a tourist town so obsessed with the Kennedys in Kurt Vonnegut's vision that even the waffles in a local restaurant are named Jackie and Caroline and Teddy. This is our Cape, too. It's the scent of sunscreen, it's damp bathing suits hung out on the line, and suppers enjoyed at the picnic table, with newspapers instead of tablecloths because eating lobster with drawn butter can be a messy undertaking. It's summer people, who flirt with each other on the ferry to Martha's Vineyard in John Cheever's story of vacation and seduction—and crowd the streets of Oak Bluffs in John Updike's memory.

On this fragile piece of land, whose great dunes were crumbling and washing away even when Thoreau visited the Highland Lighthouse of Truro, there are writers who have been lucky enough to spend a season or a lifetime. Norman Mailer and Edna St. Vincent Millay, Sylvia Plath and Paul Theroux have walked these beaches. Edgar Allan Poe has charted our storms. Herman Melville has taught us what to watch for when searching for whales. Always look to the sea, that's what we've learned out here. Some days there will be gales, other days the weather will be so mild and perfect you'll want to stare at the white clouds drifting by. You'll want to pick the roses which grow by your door, and then go down to the tide pools to study the curious and wonderful behavior of the mussels and hermit crabs. Do all these things, and then, when the light is fading and the herons are at last fishing for their supper, go home and write.

Adam Gopnik

....

On Nauset Beach

A FRIEND WRITES:

I have just returned from a week of leisure. My wife
and I decided to spend our vacation this year at a bed-and-
breakfast near Nauset beach, on Cape Cod—not the private,
genteel Cape Cod of old shingle houses and secluded sailboats
but the public, Patti Page Cape Cod of lifeguards' chairs and
Philbrick's snack shop ("On the Beach Since 1953") and enor-
mous asphalt parking lots behind the dunes which fill up by
eleven o'clock even on a weekday. Terrific place. We hadn't
been on an American beach since a drizzly summer week on

Adam Gopnik's work frequently appears in The New Yorker. He has
contributed over 100 articles and stories, including this 1988 reflection on
Thoreau, updated with the author as tourist.

that same beach eight years ago, at a gloomy time in American life when just about everything—cars, vacations, the President—seemed to be running out of gas. So we were unprepared for the pleasures of an American beach—above all, for the sheer beauty and sensuality of American bodies. "Balanchine said that America is the land of the beautiful body," my wife announced on our first day (she was reading his biography), and this seemed overwhelmingly true—especially of those blondes who, by God only knows what genetic combination, still tan to a mahogany stain. As we followed the news about the mysterious waves of hypodermic needles and broken vials that were washing up on beaches only a little to the south, Cape Cod felt not just safer but, somehow, older.

On my first day of leisure, I decided to buy a copy of Thoreau's *Cape Cod* and find out more about the history of the place. I felt extremely complacent, up on my dune, as I began reading—Thoreau seemed to me a uniquely high-minded purchase—but as the week wore on I noticed a disconcerting number of similarly pallid types perched up on the dunes with their copies of *Cape Cod*. I suspect that a copy of Thoreau's *Cape Cod* serves the same essential purpose for a particular kind of vacationer that a scrap of bikini does for the sunbathers—it establishes the high-mindedness of the owner, despite any appearances to the contrary.

Thoreau's book, I discovered, is a fine, gloomy account of several long walking tours he took on the Cape about a hundred and forty years ago. In my ignorance, I had thought that *Cape Cod* was an early book about the nascent life of leisure in America; it is in fact the direct reverse. Thoreau's purpose in going to Cape Cod was to consider what New England must have been like in its original, austere state. The Cape, for Thoreau, produces the least comfortable (and the most typically and deeply "American") people, because it is the least comfortable of places, the most uninviting landscape on earth. The book begins with corpses from a shipwreck washing up onto the shore at Cohasset, passes through the drafty cabins of older Cape Codders, and proceeds to the remote seclusion of the Highland Light. Reading Thoreau on Nauset Beach while you are actually on Nauset Beach is an eerie experience. Over there, where a family is listening to old Jefferson Airplane cassettes, is doubtless the spot where Thoreau encountered the "wrecker"—a kind of ghoulish beachcomber who collected driftwood from recent shipwrecks—and meditated on mortality. There, where two girls in one-piece mock-snakeskin swimsuits are playing paddleball, is probably the spot where Thoreau saw an earlier beach beauty he described as "a Nauset woman, of a hardness and coarseness such as no man ever possesses or suggests," adding "It was enough to see the vertebrae and sinews of her neck, and her set jaws of iron, which would have bitten a boardnail in two." And yonder, where the line for Philbrick's begins, with its happy hungry children and whining hungry children, could well be the very spot where Thoreau decided that the sea-shore is "a wild rank place . . . strewn with crabs, horse-shoes, and razor-clams, and whatever the sea casts up,—a vast morgue, where famished dogs may range in packs, and crows come daily to glean the pittance which the tide leaves them." He went on to say, "The carcasses of men and beasts together lie stately up upon its shelf, rotting and bleaching in the sun and waves, and each tide turns them in their beds, and tucks fresh sand under them. There is naked Nature,—inhumanly sincere, wasting no thought on man, nibbling at the cliffy shore where gulls wheel amid the spray."

As always happens when you are reading a good book at leisure, the author became a companion, and I started to explain to Thoreau how *that* became *this*— how that Nauset woman became these Nauset women, and how that redoubt of Puritan austerity turned into this landscape of pleasure. But Thoreau answered that what interested him was not the mechanics of this transformation but the underlying transformation in the Spirit (a word he likes to capitalize) of the place and its people. And, as the week wore on, it came to seem to us—to me and my invented Thoreau—that in some respects, at least, the Spirit of the place and its people really hadn't changed much after all. To him Nauset Beach was a hostile place that demanded a determined life, and this is still so. The people of Nauset Beach may have entirely altered their determination of what they want to do, but they haven't much altered their determination to do it, and haven't at all altered their love of determination.

The leisure of an American beach is charged with a puritanical impulse—a love of labor. A beach—any beach—is a hostile place. A suntan is yielded up by a beach as unwilling as was the paltry living the wreckers used to seek from it. Getting a tan requires patience, skill, and a feel for wind and cloud and sun as subtle as a sea captain's. (First you put up the Bain de Soleil No. 15 sunblock; then, in the middle of the day, run it down and hoist up the No. 8; leave that up and cruise through the afternoon; then take it down and track for home with the Coppertone No. 4.) There are bags and umbrellas and radios to lug and towels to shake out. There are lifeguards running races along the edge of the water all day long, back and forth, and attendants running ahead of them with bullhorns, asking everyone else to please get out of the runners' way.

This is not leisure as they know it in Europe; this is the old Pilgrim spirit finding new material to work on. What we were seeing on the beach, it seemed to us—to Thoreau and me—was not a replacement of the Puritans' vision of hostile nature and industrious man by a Mediterranean ideal of endless pleasure but something more interesting, and more authentically American: the marriage of a piety about accomplishment with the belief that the highest of all accomplishments is having a good time.

Anonymous

....

Falmouth Whaling Log

ON STATE 28, eleven miles from Mashpee. To Woods Hole, from Falmouth Green, five miles.

Sunday, Janury 9—Sixtyfore days out of Falmouth Mass & not won single whale have we tuk yit. Our Capting has ordered the man on lookout to come down, says mebbe the Lord is taking his vengints upon us for looking for whales on the Sabbith. Hear after the lookout will not go aloft no more on the Sabbith xcept oncet every our. So ends, fine wether all day.

Monday, Janury 10—Vilents broke out in the galley

This swashbuckling, anonymous account is thought to date from the early 1900s.

today. The men says they would not eat the potatoe barging becaus there was too many cockroches & other incests ect. in it, and they maid Peter White, our neegrow cook, eat it insted. So ends this day, still no whales in site.

Tuesday, Janury 11—Peter White the cook comeplaned of panes in the abdoming & died this day 3 oclock p m. The Capting has ordered the men queschinned trying to find out who is gillty of making him eat the potatoe barging, but all hands pleed innosents. So ends, not a whale in these onwholly waters.

Wensday, Janury 12—Fewnril sarvises was held at 11 a m for Peter White. All hands xept the lookout called on deck to witniss our last fairwell to our pore shipmate. He was laid in a box & the Capting begun to reed sourfully from the scripters after giveing worning that any man what udders a disrespective word is going to git seesed up in the riggin. Suddingly the lookout calls There she blows. The 1st whale we seen on the whole of this miserble viage. The Capting went on reeding over the departid & the lookout calls There she blows and breeches. Still the Skipper is reeding & the lookout calls There she blows & breeches & belches. Then the Capting drops his book and orders the men—Heave that damed carkiss overboard and lower away. But we was too late. So ends, our won whale, the only whale we seen yit—gorn.

Thursday, Janury 13—The Capting give worning this day to all hands not to die ontill we git our first whale. No fewnril sarvises will be held. So ends, not won miserble whale to be seen.

Marge Piercy

....

Homesick

FINALLY I HAVE a house

where I return.

House half into the hillside,

wood that will weather to the wind's gray,

house built on sand

drawing water like a tree from its roots

where my roots too are set

and I return.

Where the men rode crosscountry on their dirt bikes in October

---

Marge Piercy makes her home in Wellfleet with her novelist husband Ira Wood. Much of her poetry and fiction is filled with the imagery of the Cape, including this poem from her 1976 collection, Living in the Open.

the hog cranberry will not grow back.
This land is vulnerable like my own flesh.
In New York the land seems cast out by a rolling mill
except where ancient gneiss pokes through.
Plains and mountains dwarf the human, seeming permanent,
but Indians were chasing mammoth with Folsom points
before glacial debris piled up Cape Cod where I return.

The colonists found beech and oak trees high as steeples
and chopped them down.
When Thoreau hiked from Sandwich outward
he crossed a desert
for they had farmed the land until it blew away
and slaughtered the whales and seals extinct.

Here you must make the frail dirt where your food grows.
Fertility is created of human castings and the sea's.
In the intertidal beach around each sand grain
swims a minute world dense with life.
Each oil slick wipes out galaxies.
Here we all lie on the palm of the poisoned sea our mother
where life began and is now ending
and we return.

Norman Mailer

....

Tough Guys Don't Dance

AT DAWN, IF it was low tide on the flats, I would awaken
to the chatter of gulls. On a bad morning, I used to feel as if
I had died and the birds were feeding on my heart. Later,
after I had dozed for a while, the tide would come up over
the sand as swiftly as a shadow descends on the hills when
the sun lowers behind the ridge, and before long the first
swells would pound on the bulkhead of the deck below my
bedroom window, the shock rising in one fine fragment of
time from the sea wall to the innermost passages of my flesh.

---

*Novelist and journalist Norman Mailer is the author of a string of best-selling
tomes, including* The Armies of the Night, The Executioner's Song *and*
The Naked and the Dead. *His 1984 novel,* Tough Guys Don't Dance,
is a psychological murder mystery set on the Cape.

Boom! the waves would go against the wall, and I could have been alone on a freighter on a dark sea.

In fact, I was awakening alone in bed, on the twenty-fourth drear morning after my wife had decamped. That evening, still alone, I would celebrate the twenty-fourth night. It must have proved quite an occasion. Over days to come, when I would be searching for a clue to my several horrors, I would attempt to peer through the fog-banks of memory to recall just what acts I might or might not have committed on all of that twenty-fourth night.

Little came back to me, however, of what I did after I got out of bed. It may have been a day like all the others. There is a joke about a man who is asked on his first visit to a new doctor to describe his daily routine. He promptly offers: "I get up, I brush my teeth, I vomit, I wash my face . . ." at which point the doctor inquires, "You vomit every day?"

"Oh, yes, Doctor," replies the patient. "Doesn't everyone?"

I was that man. Each morning, after breakfast, I could not light a cigarette. I had no more than to put one in my mouth and was ready to retch. The foul pleni-tude of losing a wife was embracing me.

For twelve years I had been trying to give up smoking. As Mark Twain said—and who does not know the remark?—"It's nothing to stop. I've quit a hundred times." I used to feel I had said it myself, for certainly I had tried on ten times ten occasions, once for a year, once for nine months, once for four months. Over and over again I gave them up, a hundred times over the years, but always I went back. For in my dreams, sooner or later, I struck a match, brought flame to the tip, then took in all my hunger for existence with the first puff. I felt impaled on desire itself—those fiends trapped in my chest and screaming for one drag. Change the given!

So I learned what addiction is. A beast had me by the throat and its vitals were in my lungs. I wrestled that devil for twelve years and sometimes I beat him back. Usually it was at great loss to myself, and great loss to others. For when I did not smoke, I grew violent. My reflexes lived in the place where the match used to strike, and my mind would lose those bits of knowledge that keep us serene (at least if we are American). In the throes of not smoking, I might rent a car and never notice whether it was a Ford or a Chrysler. That can be seen as the beginning of the end. On one occasion, when I did not smoke, I went on a long trip with a girl I loved named Madeleine to meet up with a married couple who wanted to have a weekend of wife-swapping. We indulged them. Driving back, Madeleine and I had a quarrel, and I wrecked the car. Madeleine's insides were badly hurt. I went back to smoking.

I used to say: "It's easier to give up the love of your life than to kick cigarettes," and suspect I was right in such a remark. But then last month, twenty-four days ago, my wife took off. Twenty-four days ago. I learned a little more about addiction. It may be simpler to give up love than dispense with your smokes, but when it comes to saying goodbye to love-and-hate—ah, that reliable standby of the head shrinkers, the love-hate relationship!—why, ending your marriage is easily as difficult as relinquishing your nicotine, and much the same, for I can tell you that after twelve years, I had gotten to hate the filthy stuff just so much as a bitter wife. Even the first inhale of the morning (whose sure bliss once seemed the ineradicable reason I could never give up tobacco) had now become a convulsion of coughing. No more might remain than the addiction itself, but addiction is still a signature on the bottom line of your psyche.

That is how it was with my marriage, now that Patty Lareine was gone. If I had loved her once while knowing her frightful faults—even as we smoke like happy fiends and shrug away the thought of a lung cancer still decades away, so did I always perceive that Patty Lareine could be my doom around the bend of some treacherous evening—yet, so be it, I adored her. Who knew? Love might inspire us to transcend our dire fevers. That was years ago. Now, for the last year and more, we had been trying to kick the habit of each other. Intimate detestations had grown each season until they rooted out all the old pockets of good humor. I had come to dislike her as much as my morning cigarette. Which, indeed, I had at last given up. After twelve years, I felt finally free of the largest addiction of my life. That is, until the night she left. That was the night I discovered that losing my wife was a heavier trip.

Before her departure, I had not had a cigarette for all of a year. Patty Lareine and I might, on the consequence, fight ferociously, but I was quits at last with my Camels. Small hope. Two hours after she drove off, I took up one coffin nail from a half-empty pack Patty left behind, and was, in two days of battling myself, hooked once again. Now that she was gone, I began each day with the most horrendous convulsion of my spirit. God, I choked in cataracts of misery. For with the return of this bummer habit came back every bit of the old longing for Patty Lareine. Each cigarette smelled in my mouth like an ashtray, but it was not tar I sniffed, rather my own charring flesh. Such is the odor of funk and loss.

Well, as I indicated, I do not remember how I spent my Twenty-fourth Day. My clearest recollection is yawping over that first cigarette, strangling the smoke down. Later, after four or five, I was sometimes able to inhale in peace, thereby cauterizing what I had come to decide (with no great respect for myself) must be the wound of my life. How much more I longed for Patty Lareine than I wished to. In those twenty-four days I did my best to see no one, I stayed at home, I did not always wash, I drank as if the great river of our blood is carried by bourbon, not water, I was—to put a four-letter word on it—a mess.

In summer it might have been more obvious to others what a sorry hour I was in, but this was late in the fall, the days were gray, the town deserted, and on many a shortening November afternoon you could have taken a bowling ball and rolled it down the long one-way lane of our narrow main street (a true New England alley) without striking a pedestrian or a car. The town withdrew into itself, and the cold, which was nothing remarkable when measured with a thermometer (since the seacoast off Massachusetts is, by Fahrenheit, less frigid than the stony hills west of Boston) was nonetheless a cold sea air filled with the bottomless chill that lies at the cloistered heart of ghost stories. Or, indeed, at many a séance. In truth, there had been a séance Patty and I attended at the end of September with disconcerting results: short and dreadful, it ended with a shriek. I suspect that part of the reason I was now bereft of Patty Lareine was that something intangible but indisputably repulsive had attached itself to our marriage in that moment.

After she left, there was a week when the weather never shifted. One chill morose November sky went into another. The place turned gray before one's eyes. Back in summer, the population had been thirty thousand and doubled on weekends. It seemed as if every vehicle on Cape Cod chose to drive down the four-lane state highway that ended at our beach. Provincetown was as colorful then as St. Tropez, and as dirty by Sunday evening as Coney Island. In the fall, however, with everyone gone, the town revealed its other presence. Now the population did not boil up daily from thirty thousand to sixty, but settled down to its honest sediment, three thousand souls, and on empty weekday afternoons you might have said the true number of inhabitants must be thirty men and women, all hiding.

There could be no other town like it. If you were sensitive to crowds, you might expire in summer from human propinquity. On the other hand, if you were unable to endure loneliness, the vessel of your person could fill with dread during the long winter. Martha's Vineyard, not fifty miles to the south and west, had lived through the upsurge of mountains and their erosion, through the rise and fall of oceans, the life and death of great forests and swamps. Dinosaurs had passed over Martha's Vineyard, and their bones were compacted into the bedrock. Glaciers had come and gone, sucking the island to the north, pushing it like a ferry to the south again. Martha's Vineyard had fossil deposits one million centuries old. The northern reach of Cape Cod, however, on which my house sat, the land I inhabited—that long curving spit of shrub and dune that curves in upon itself in a spiral at the tip of the Cape—had only been formed by wind and sea over the last ten thousand years. That cannot amount to more than a night of geological time.

Perhaps this is why Provincetown is so beautiful. Conceived at night (for one would swear it was created in the course of one dark storm) its sand flats still glistened in the dawn with the moist primeval innocence of land exposing itself to the sun for the first time. Decade after decade, artists came to paint the light of Provincetown, and comparisons were made to the lagoons of Venice and the marshes of Holland, but then the summer ended and most of the painters left, and the long dingy undergarment of the gray New England winter, gray as the spirit of my mood, came down to visit. One remembered then that the land was only ten thousand years old, and one's ghosts had no roots. We did not have old Martha's Vineyard's fossil remains to subdue each spirit, no, there was nothing to domicile our specters who careened with the wind down the two long streets of our town which curved together around the bay like two spinsters on their promenade to church.

If this is a fair sample of how my mind worked on the Twenty-fourth Day, it is obvious I was feeling introspective, long-moldering, mournful and haunted. Twenty-four days of being without a wife you love and hate and certainly fear is guaranteed to leave you cleaving to her like the butt end of addiction itself. How I hated the taste of cigarettes now that I was smoking again.

It seems to me that I walked the length of the town that day and back again to my house—her house— it was Patty Lareine's money that had bought our home. Three miles along Commercial Street I walked, and back through all the shank of that gray afternoon, but I do not remember whom I spoke to, nor how many or few might have passed in a car and invited me to ride. No, I remember I walked to the very end of town, out to where the last house meets the place on the beach where the Pilgrims first landed in America. Yes, it was not at Plymouth but *here* that they landed.

I contemplate the event on many a day. Those Pilgrims, having crossed the Atlantic, encountered the cliffs of Cape Cod as their first sight of land. On that back shore the surf, at its worst, can break in waves ten feet high. On windless days the peril is worse; a sailing vessel can be driven in by the relentless tides to founder on the shoals. It is not the rocks but the shifting sands that sink you off Cape Cod. What fear those Pilgrims must have known on hearing the dull eternal boom of the surf. Who would dare come near that shore with boats such as theirs? They turned south, and the white deserted coast remained unrelenting—no hint of a cove. Just the long straight beach. So they tried going to the north and in a day saw the shore bent west, then continue to curve until it turned to the south. What trick of the land was this? Now they were sailing to the east, three quarters of the way around from the north. Were they circumnavigating an ear of the sea? They came around the point, and dropped anchor in the lee. It was a natural harbor, as protected, indeed, as the inside of one's ear. From there, they put down small boats and rowed to shore. A plaque commemorates the landing. It is by the beginning of the breakwater that now protects our marshes at the end of town from the final ravages of the sea. There is where you come to the end of the road, to the farthest place a tourist can ride out toward the tip of Cape Cod and encounter the landing place of the Pilgrims. It was only weeks later, after much bad weather and the recognition that there was little game to hunt and few fields to till in these sandy lands, that the Pilgrims sailed west across the bay to Plymouth.

Here, however, was were they first landed with all the terror and exaltation of encountering the new land. New land it was, not ten thousand years old. A strew of sand. How many Indian ghosts must have howled through the first nights of their encampment.

I think of the Pilgrims whenever I walk to these emerald-green marshes at the end of town. Beyond, the coastal dunes are so low that one can see ships along the horizon even when the water is not visible. The flying bridges of sport-fishing boats seem to travel in caravans along the sand. If I have a drink in me, I begin to laugh, because across from the plaque to the Pilgrims, not fifty yards away, there where the United States began, stands the entrance to a huge motel. If it is no uglier than any other vast motel, it is certainly no prettier, and the only homage the Pilgrims get is that it is called an Inn. Its asphalt parking lot is as large as a football field. Pay homage to the Pilgrims.

No more than this, no matter how I press and force my mind, is what I remember of how I spent my Twenty-fourth afternoon. I went out, I walked across the town, I brooded on the geology of our shores, loaned my imagination to the Pilgrims, and laughed at the Provincetown Inn. Then I suppose I must have walked on home. The gloom in which I lay in the grasp of my sofa was timeless. I had spent many hours in these twenty-four days staring at the wall, but what I do recollect, what I cannot ignore, is that in the evening I got into my Porsche and drove up Commercial Street very slowly, as if afraid that this night I might run into a child—the evening was foggy—and I did not stop until I came to The Widow's Walk. There, not far from the Provincetown Inn, is a dark stained pine-paneled room whose foundations are gently slapped in the rising of the tide, for one of the charms of Provincetown I have neglected to pass along is that not only my house—her house!—but most of the buildings on the bay side of Commercial Street are kin to ships at high tide when the bulkheads on which they rest are half submerged by the sea.

It was such a tide tonight. The waters rose as languorously as if we were in the tropics, but I knew the sea was cold. Behind the good windows of this dark room, the fire on its wide hearth was worthy of a postcard, and my wooden chair was full of approaching winter, inasmuch as it had a shelf of the kind they used in study halls a hundred years ago: a large round platter of oak lifted on its hinges to enable you to sit down, after which it ensconced itself under your right elbow to serve as a table for your drink.

The Widow's Walk might as well have been created for me. On lonely fall evenings I liked to entertain the conceit that I was some modern tycoon-pirate of prodigious wealth who kept the place for his amusement. The large restaurant at the other end might be rarely entered by me, but the small bar of this paneled lounge equipped with its barmaid was all for myself. Secretly I must have believed that no one else had a right to enter. By November, the illusion was not difficult to protect. On quiet weekday nights most of the diners, good senior Wasps from Brewster and Dennis and Orleans, out for a smack of excitement, found their thrills in the sheer audacity of daring to drive all of thirty or forty miles to Provincetown itself. The echo of summer kept our evil reputation intact. Those fine Scotch studies in silver—

which is to say, each Wasp professor emeritus and retired corporate executive—did not look to tarry in a bar. They headed for the Dining Room. Besides, one look at me in my dungaree jacket was enough to steer them to the food. "No, dear," their wives would say, "let's have our drinks at the table. We're starved!"

"Yeah, baby" I would murmur to myself, "starved."

Over these twenty-four days, the Lounge at The Widow's Walk had become my castle keep. I would sit by the window, study the fire, and watch the changes in the tide, feeling after four bourbons, ten cigarettes, and a dozen crackers with cheese (my dinner!) that I was, at least, a wounded lord living by the sea.

The compensation for misery, self-pity, and despair is that fed enough drinks, the powers of imagination return with force. No matter that they are lopsided under such auspices; they return. In this room my drinks were well stoked by a submissive bar girl doubtless terrified of me although I never said anything more provocative than "Another bourbon, please." Yet, since she worked in a bar, I understood her fear. I had worked in a bar myself for many years. I could respect her conviction that I was dangerous. That was apparent in the concentration of my good manners. In the days when I used to be a bartender, I had watched over a few customers like myself. They never bothered you until they did. Then the room could get smashed.

I did not see myself as belonging to such a category. But how could I say that the waitress' dire expectation did not serve me well? I received no more attention than I wanted and every bit I might need. The manager, a young and pleasant fellow, much set on maintaining the tone of the establishment, had now known me for more than a few years, and as long as I had been accompanied by my rich wife, considered me a rare example of local gentry no matter how obstreperous Patty Lareine might get on drink: Wealth is worth that much! Now that I was by myself, he greeted me when I came in, said goodbye when I went out, and had obviously made the proprietorial decision to leave me strictly alone. As a corollary, few visitors were steered into the Lounge. Night after night, I could get drunk in the manner I chose.

Not until now have I been ready to confess that I am a writer. From Day One, however, no new writing had been done, not in more than three weeks. To see one's situation as ironic is, we may agree, no joy, but irony becomes a dungeon when the circle is closed. The cigarettes I gave up at such cost to my ability to write had, on this last return to the domain of nicotine—it is no less than a domain—cut off all ability to come forth with even one new paragraph. In order not to smoke, I had had to learn to write all over again. Now that I could manage such a feat, the return to cigarettes seemed to have tamped out every literary spark. Or was it the departure of Patty Lareine?

These days I would take my notebook with me to The Widow's Walk, and when drunk enough, would succeed in adding a line or two to words I had set down in less desperate hours. On those random occasions, therefore, when visitors were actually sharing a predinner drink in the same public room with me, my small sounds of appreciation at some felicity of syntax or my bored grunts before a phrase that now seemed as dead as an old drinking friend's repetitions must have sounded strange and animal, as unsettling (given the paneled gentility of this Lounge) as cries made by a hound absolutely indifferent to any nearby human presence.

Can I claim I was not playing to the house when I would frown over a drunken note I could hardly read, and then chuckle in pleasure as soon as these alcoholic squiggles metamorphosed into a legible text? "There," I would mutter to myself, "studies!"

I had just made out part of a title, a bona-fide title, sufficiently resonant for a book: In Our Wild—Studies among the Sane by Timothy Madden.

Now, an exegesis commenced on my name. In Our Wild—Studies among the Sane by Mac Madden? By Tim Mac Madden? By Two-Mac Madden? I began to giggle. My waitress, poor overalerted mouse, was able to flick a look at me only by setting herself resolutely in profile.

Yet I was giggling truly. Old jokes about my name were returning. I felt one rush of love for my father. Ah, the sweet sorrow of loving a parent. It is as pure as the taste of a sourball when you are five. Douglas "Dougy" Madden—Big Mac to his friends and to his only child, myself, once called Little Mac, or Mac-Mac, then Two-Mac and Toomey and back to Tim. Following the morphology of my name through the coils of booze, I giggled. Each change of my name had been an event in my life—if I could only recover the events.

In my heart I was now trying to launch a first set of phrases for the initial essay. (What a title! In Our Wild—Studies among the Sane by Tim Madden.) I might speak of the Irish and the reason they drink so much. Could it be the testosterone? The Irish presumably had more than other men, my father did for certain, and it made them unmanageable. Maybe the hormone asked to be dissolved in some liquor.

I sat with pencil poised, my sip of bourbon near to scorching my tongue. I was not ready to swallow. This title was about all that had come to me since Day One. I could merely ponder the waves. The waves outside the lounge-room window on this chill November night had become equal in some manner to the waves in my mind. My thoughts came to a halt and I felt the disappointment of profound drunken vision. Just as you waddle up to the true relations of the cosmos, your vocabulary blurs.

It was then I grew aware that I was no longer
alone in my realm of The Widow's Walk. A blonde
remarkably like Patty Lareine was sitting with her escort
not ten feet away. If I had no other clue to the profound submersions of my conscious state, it was enough
that she had entered with her bucko, a nicely tailored
country-tweed-and-flannels, silver-winged-pompadour,
suntanned-lawyer-type fellow, yes, the lady had sat
down with her sheik, and since they now had drinks in
front of them, must have been talking (and in unabashed
voices, hers at least) for a considerable period. Five minutes? Ten minutes? I realized that they had sized me up,
and for whatever reason, had the confidence, call it the
gall, to ignore me. Whether this insularity derived from
some not easily visible proficiency the man might call
upon in the martial arts—Tweed-and-Flannels looked
more like a tennis player than a Black Belt—or whether
they were so wealthy a couple that nothing unpleasant
ever walked up to them in the way of strangers (unless it
was burglary of the mansion) or whether they were
exhibiting simple insensitivity to the charged torso, head
and limbs sitting so near them, I do not know, but the
woman, at least, was talking loudly, and as if I did not
exist. What an insult at this beleaguered hour!

Then I understood. From their conversation I
could soon divine that they were Californians, just as
loose and unselfconscious in deportment as tourists from

New Jersey visiting a bar in Munich. What could they
know of how they were degrading me?

As my attention went through those ponderous
maneuvers of which only a human in deep depression
can speak—the brain lurches like an elephant backed into
its stall—I climbed at last out of the dungeon of my
massive self-absorption to take a look at them, and
thereby came to realize that their indifference to me was
neither arrogance, confidence, nor innocence but, to the
contrary, theatrical to the hilt. A set of poses. The man
was highly keyed to the likelihood that a glowering presence such as mine was hardly to be ignored as a source
of real trouble, and the woman, true to my premise that
blondes believe it obscene not to comport themselves as
angels or bitches—each option must be equally avail-
able—was stampeding along. She wished to provoke me.
She wanted to test her beau's courage. No mean surro-
gate was this lady for my own Patty Lareine.

But let me describe the woman. It's worth the
look. She must have been fifteen years older than my
wife, and thereby, not far from fifty, but what a splen-
did approach! There used to be a porny star named
Jennifer Welles who had the same appearance. She had
large, well-turned promiscuous breasts—one nipple tilted
to the east, one stared out to the west—a deep navel, a
woman's round belly, a sweet buoyant spread of but-
tocks, and dark pubic hair. That was what encouraged the

prurience to stir in those who bought a ticket to watch
Jennifer Welles. Any lady who chooses to become a
blonde is truly a blonde.

Now, the face of my new neighbor was, like the
porny star, Jennifer Welles, undeniably appealing. She
had a charming upturned nose and a full pout on the
mouth, as spoiled and imperious as the breath of sex.
Her nostrils flared, her fingernails—the Liberation could
go screw itself!—were scandalously well-manicured with
a silver varnish to catch the silver-blue toning above her
eyes. What a piece! An anachronism. The most complacent kind of West Coast money. Santa Barbara? La Jolla?
Pasadena? Wherever it was, she must certainly come
from an enclave of bridge players. Perfectly groomed
blondes remain as quintessential to such places as mus-
tard on pastrami. Corporate California had moved right
into my psyche.

I can hardly describe what an outrage this
seemed. As well paste a swastika outside the office of
the United Jewish Appeal. This blonde reminded me
so directly of Patty Lareine that I felt obliged to strike.
Do what? I could hardly say. At the very least, gore
their mood.

So I listened. She was one immaculately dressed
full-bodied lady who liked to drink. She could take them
back to back. Scotch, of course. Chivas Regal. "Chivvies,"
she called them. "Miss," she told the waitress, "give me

another Chivvies. Lots of diamonds." That was her word for ice, ha, ha.

"Of course you're bored with me," she said to her man in a loud and most self-certain voice, as if she could measure to the drop just how much sex she might be sitting upon. A powerhouse. There are voices that resonate into one's secret strings like tuning forks. Hers was one. It is crude to say, but one would do much for such a voice. There was always the hope that its moist little relative below would offer something of the same for your preserves.

Patty Lareine had such a voice. She could be diabolical with her lip around a Very Dry Martini (which, of course, count on it, she would insist on calling a Marty Seco). "It was gin," she'd say in all the husky enthusiasm of her hot-to-trot larynx, "it was gin as done the old lady in. Yes, asshole," oh, and she would include you most tenderly in this jeer, as if, by God, even you, asshole, could feel all right if you were being kept around her. But then, Patty Lareine belonged to another kind of wealth, strictly derivative. Her second husband, Meeks Wardley Hilby III (whom once she most certainly tried to persuade me to murder) was old Tampa money and she drilled him good but not between the eyes, rather up his financial fundament thanks to her divorce lawyer, a whiz bomb (who, I used to assume to my pain, was probably massaging the back wall of her belly every night for a time, but then, one cannot expect less of a dedicated divorce lawyer—it pays off in presenting the witness). Although Patty Lareine was trim to bursting in her build, and in those days, peppy as a spice jar, he modulated the moxie of her personality down to more delicate herbs. With the aid of intense coaching (he was one of the first to use a video camera for rehearsal) he showed her how to be tremulous on the stand and thereby turn the judgmental eye into—forgive me!—one fat old judge melting away. Before they were done, her marital peccadilloes (and her husband had witnesses) came out as the maidenly mistakes of a desperately beleaguered and much abused fine lady. Each ex-lover appearing as witness against her was depicted as one more unhappy attempt to cure the heart that her husband had shattered. Patty may have begun life as one good high school cheerleader, just a little old redneck from a down-home North Carolina town, but by the time she was ready to divorce Wardley (and marry me) she had developed a few social graces. Hell, her lawyer and she grew equal to Lunt and Fontanne in the manner they could pass a bowl of soup back and forth on the witness stand. One scion of old Gulf Coast Florida money was certainly divested of a share of his principal. That was how Patty came to belong to wealth.

The more I listened to the lady in The Widow's Walk, however, the more I could discern that she was of other ilk. Patty's wits were true wit—that was all she had to stand between her and the crass and crude. This new blonde lady now transforming my evening might be short on wit, but then, she had small need for it. Her manner came with her money. If all else was right, she would probably meet you at her hotel-room door attired in no more than white elbow-length gloves. (And high heels.)

"Go ahead, say you're bored," I now heard clearly. "It's to be expected when an attractive man and woman decide to go on a trip. To be thrown together for all these days creates the fear of disenchantment. Tell me if I'm wrong."

It was obvious that her interest in his reply was less than her pleasure in letting me know that they not only were not married, but were, by anyone's estimate, on a quick and limited fling. It could wrap itself up on any turn. Taken as a beast on the hoof, Tweed-and-Flannels shouldn't be too hard to replace for a one-night stand. This lady had a body language to suggest that you would be given one thoroughgoing welcome on first night—only later would difficulties arise. But the first night would be on the house.

No, I'm not bored, Tweed-and-Flannels was telling her now in the lowest voice, not bored at all, his voice droning into her ear like white noise put on the audio system to dull your synapses to sleep. Yes, I

decided, he must be a lawyer. There was something in
the confidential moderation of his manner. He was
addressing the Bench on a point of law, helping the
judge not to blow the case. Soothing!

Her text, however, was obstreperous! "No, no,
no," she said, giving a light shake to her ice cubes, "it
was my idea we come here. Your negotiations take you
to Boston, well then, I said, my whim also takes me. Do
you mind? Of course you don't. Daddy is mad about
brand-new mama. Et cetera," she said, pausing for a sip
of the Chivvies. "But, darling, I have this vice. I can't
bear contentment. The moment I feel it, everything says
'Goodbye, my dear!' Moreover, I'm an avid map reader,
as you have learned, Lonnie. They say women can't read
directions. I can. At Kansas City, way back in—wait, it
comes to me—in 1976, I was the only Jerry Ford
woman in our delegation who could read a map well
enough to drive from the hotel to his headquarters.

"So, there was your mistake. Showing me a map
of Boston and its environs. When you hear that tone in
my voice, when I say, 'Darling, I'd like to see a map of
this region,' beware. It means my toes are itching.
Lonnie, ever since I was in the fifth grade and started
geography studies"—she squinted critically at the melting diamonds in her glass—"I used to stare at Cape Cod
on the map of New England. It sticks out like a pinkie.
You know how children are about pinkies? That's their

little finger, the one close to them. So I wanted to see the tip of Cape Cod."

I must say I still didn't like her friend. He had that much-massaged look of a man whose money makes money while he sleeps. Not at all, not at all, he was telling her, laying his salad oil on her stirred-up little sorrows, we both wanted to come here, it's truly all right, and more of such, and more of such.

"No, Lonnie, I gave you no choice. I was a tyrant about it. I said, 'I want to go to this place, Province-town.' I wouldn't allow you to demur. So here we are. It's a whim on top of a whim, and you're bored stiff. You want to drive back to Boston tonight. This place is deserted, right?"

At this point—make no mistake about it—she looked at me full out: full of welcome if I took it up, full of scorn in the event I did not reply.

I spoke. I said to her, "That's what you get for trusting a map."

It must have worked. For my next recollection is of sitting with them. I may as well confess that my memory is damnable. What I recall, I see clearly—some-times!—but often I cannot connect the events of a night. So my next recollection is of sitting with them. I must have been invited over. I must, indeed, have been good company. Even he was laughing. Leonard Pangborn was his name, Lonnie Pangborn, a good family name in

Republican California, doubtless—and hers was not Jennifer Welles but Jessica Pond. Pond and Pangborn— can you understand my animosity now? They had the patina that comes off a TV screen from characters in a soap opera.

Actually, I began to entertain her considerably. I think it is because I had not spoken to anyone for days. Now, depression or no, some buried good humor in me seemed well rested. I began to relate a few stories about the Cape, and my timing was vigorous. I must have been as energetic as a convict on a one-day pass outside the walls, but then, I was so well on my way to getting along with Pond that it came near to lifting me out of my doldrums. For one thing, I soon divined that she was drawn to substantial property. Fine mansions on good green lawns with high wrought-iron gates gave her the same glow a real estate agent derives from bringing the right client to the right house. Of course, I soon figured it out. To the money she was born with, Jessica had added her own pile. Back in California she was exactly that, a successful country real estate agent.

What a disappointment Provincetown must have been to her. We offer our indigenous architecture, but it is funky: old fish-shed with wooden-stairway-on-the-outside Cape Cod salt-box. We sell room-space to tourists. One hundred rented rooms can end up having one hundred outside stairways. Provincetown, to anyone looking for gracious living, is no more uncluttered than twenty telephone poles at a crossroads.

Maybe she was deceived by the delicacy of our site on the map: the fine filigree tip of the Cape curls around itself like the toe of a medieval slipper? Probably she had pictured swards of lawn. Instead, she had to look at honkytonk shops boarded up and a one-way main street so narrow that if a truck was parked at the curb, you held your breath and hoped nothing scratched your rented sedan as you went on through.

Naturally, she asked me about the most imposing house our town can point to. It sits on a hill, a five-story château—the only one in town—and is fenced about in high wrought iron. It is far removed from its gate. I couldn't say who lived there now, or whether he owned or rented. I had heard the name and forgot. It is not easy to explain to strangers, but in the winter, people choose to burrow down in Provincetown. Getting to know new arrivals is no simpler than traveling from island to island. Besides, none of my acquaintances, dressed as we were for winter (dungarees, boots and parkas) would ever get past a gate. I assumed that the present seigneur of our one imposing house had to be some kind of rich gink. So I drew on the rich man I knew best (who happened, indeed, to be Patty Lareine's ex-husband from Tampa) and I moved him all the way north to Provincetown and loaned him the château. I did not wish to lose momentum with Miss Jessica.

"Oh, that place belongs," I said, "to Meeks Wardley Hilby the Third. He lives all alone there." I paused. "I used to know him. We went to Exeter at the same time."

"Oh," said Jessica after quite a pause, "do you think we could pay him a visit?"

"He's not there now. He rarely stays in town any longer."

"Too bad," she said.

"You wouldn't like him," I told her. "He's a very odd fellow. At Exeter he used to drive all the deans crazy by tweaking the dress code. We had to wear jackets and ties to class, but old Wardley would get himself up like a prince of the Salvation Army."

There must have been some promise in my voice, for she began to laugh happily, but I remember that even as I began to tell her more I had the strongest feeling I should not go on—just as irrational as an unaccountable smell of smoke—do you know, I sometimes think we are all of us equal to broadcasting stations and some stories should not be put on the air. Let us leave it that I had an unmistakable injunction not to continue (which I knew I would ignore—that much is to be said for an attractive blonde!) and at the moment, even as I looked for the next words, an image came to me across the years, bright as a coin from the mint, of Meeks Wardley Hilby III, of *Wardley*, gangling along in his chinos, his patent-leather pumps and his old dinner jacket that he wore every day to class (to the consternation of half the faculty), his satin lapels faded and scuffed, his purple socks and heliotrope bow tie standing out like neon signs in Vegas.

"God," I said to Jessica, "we used to call him 'goon-child.' "

"You have to tell me all about him," she said. "Please."

"I don't know," I replied. "The story has its sordid touches."

"Oh, do tell us," said Pangborn.

I hardly needed encouragement. "Attribute it to the father," I said. "There has to be a powerful influence coming from the father. He's dead now. Meeks Wardley Hilby the Second."

"How do you tell them apart?" asked Pangborn.

"Well, they always called the father Meeks and the son Wardley. There was no confusion."

"Ah," he said. "Were they at all alike?"

"Not much. Meeks was a sportsman and Wardley was Wardley. In childhood, the nurses used to tie his hands to the bed. Meek's orders. It was calculated to put a stop to Wardley's onanism." I looked at her as if to say, "This is the detail I was afraid of." She gave a smile, which I took to mean, "We're by the fire. Tell your tale."

I did. I worked at it with great care, and gave them a full account of the adolescence of Meeks Wardley

Hilby III, never stopping to chide myself for this outrageous change of venue from the palace on the Gulf Coast to the northern estate here on the hill, but then, this was only Pond and Pangborn I was telling it to. What would they care, I told myself, where it took place?

So I went on. Meeks's wife, Wardley's mother, was sickly, and Meeks took a mistress. Wardley's mother died when he was in his first year at Exeter, and soon after, the father married the mistress. Neither of them ever liked Wardley. He liked them no better. Since they kept a door locked on the third floor of their house, Wardley decided that was the room to get into. Not, however, until he was kicked out of Exeter in his last year was he ever home long enough to find his father and the new wife away for a night. On the first evening that that happened, he worked himself up sufficiently to inch along an exterior molding of the mansion's wall three stories up from the ground, and went in through the window.

"I love this," said Jessica. "What was in the room?"

He discovered, I told her, a large old-fashioned view camera with a black cloth, mounted on a heavy tripod in one corner, and on a library table, five red vellum scrapbooks. It was a special pornographic collection. The five scrapbooks contained large sepia photographs of Meeks making love to his mistress.

"The one who was now the wife?" asked Pangborn.

I nodded. As described by the son, the first pictures must have been taken in the year Wardley was born. Each successive volume of the scrapbooks showed the father and mistress getting older. A year or two after the death of Wardley's mother, not long after the new marriage, another man appeared in the photos. "He was the manager of the estate," I said. "Wardley told me that he dined with the family every day."

At this point Lonnie clapped her hands together. "Incredible," he said.

The later photographs showed the manager making love to the wife while the father sat five feet away reading a newspaper. The lovers would adopt different positions but Meeks kept reading the paper.

"Who was the photographer?" Jessica asked.

"Wardley said it was the butler."

"What a house!" Jessica exclaimed. "Only in New England could this occur." We all laughed a great deal at that.

I did not add that the butler seduced Wardley at the age of fourteen. Nor did I offer Wardley's statement on the matter: "I've spent the rest of my life trying to regain property rights to my rectum." There was probably a fine line of propriety to tread with Jessica. I had not found it yet, so I was cautious. "At nineteen," I said, "Wardley got married. I think it was to confound his father. Meeks was a confirmed anti-Semite and the bride was a Jewish girl. She also happened to have a large nose."

They enjoyed this so much that I felt a few regrets at going on, but no helping it now—I also had the ruthlessness of the storyteller and the next detail was crucial. "This nose," I said, "as Wardley described it, curled over her upper lip until she looked as if she were breathing the fumes of her mouth. For some reason, maybe because he was a gourmet, this was indescribably carnal to Wardley."

"Oh, I hope it turned out all right," remarked Jessica.

"Well, not exactly," I said. "Wardley's wife had been well brought up. So, woe to Wardley when she discovered that he, too, had a pornography collection. She destroyed it. Then she made it worse. She managed to charm the father. After five years of marriage she succeeded in pleasing Meeks enough for the old man to give a dinner party for his son and daughter-in-law. Wardley got very drunk, and later that night, brained his wife with a candlestick. She happened to die from the blow."

"Oh, no," said Jessica. "It all took place in that house on the hill?"

"Yes."

"What," asked Pangborn, "was the legal upshot?"

"Well, believe it if you will, they did not use insanity for a defense."

"Then he must have done some time."

"He did." I was not about to mention that we had not only gone to Exeter together but actually met each other again in the same prison at the same time.

"It sounds to me as if the father was directing his son's case," said Lonnie.

"I think you're right."

"Of course! With a plea of insanity, the defense would have had to bring the scrapbooks into court." Lonnie locked his fingers together and flexed them outward. "So," he said, "Wardley took the fall. What was going to jail worth to him?"

"One million dollars a year," I answered. "Put in a trust fund each year for each year he served, plus a split with his stepmother on the estate after the father's death."

"Do you know for a fact whether they paid it over to him?" Lonnie asked.

Jessica shook her head. "I don't see such people honoring their agreement."

I shrugged. "Meeks paid," I told them, "because Wardley had filched the scrapbooks. Believe me, when Meeks died, the Stepmother kept the bargain. Meeks Wardley Hilby the Third came out of jail a wealthy man."

Jessica said, "I love how you tell a story."

Pangborn nodded. "Priceless," he said.

She was pleased. The trip to this strange place

seemed to have come to a few good minutes, after all. "Does Wardley," she asked, "plan to live in the house again?"

I was hesitating what to say to this when Pangborn replied, "Of course not. Our new friend here has made it all up."

"Well, Leonard," I said, "remind me to hire you if I need a lawyer."

"Did you make it up?" she asked.

I was not about to give a small smile and say, "Some of it." Instead I said, "Yes. Every last drop," and emptied my drink. Leonard, doubtless, had already made his inquiries about who owned the estate.

My next recollection is that I was alone again. They had gone into the dining room.

I remember drinking, and writing, and watching the water. Some observations I would put in my pocket and some I would rip up. The sound of paper as it was being torn set off reverberations in me. I began to chortle within. I was thinking that surgeons had to be the happiest people on earth. To cut people up and get paid for it—that's happiness, I told myself. It made me with Jessica Pond was next to me once more. She might have given a glad howl at the thought.

It comes back to me that I then wrote a longer note which I found in my pocket the next day. For some reason I gave it a title: RECOGNITION. "The perception of the possibility of greatness in myself has always been followed by desire to murder the nearest unworthy." Then I underlined the next sentence: "It is better to keep a modest notion of oneself!"

The more, however, that I read this note, the more I seemed to install myself in that impregnable hauteur which is, perhaps, the most satisfying aspect of solitary drinking. The knowledge that Jessica Pond and Leonard Pangborn were sitting at a table not a hundred feet away, oblivious to what might be their considerable peril, had an intoxicating effect on me, and I began to contemplate—I must say it was with no serious passion, rather as one more variety of amusing myself through another night—how easy it would be to do away with them. Consider it! After twenty-four days without Patty Lareine, this is the sort of man I had become!

Here was my reasoning. A clandestine couple, each of whom is obviously well-placed in whatever world they inhabit in California, decide to go to Boston together. They are discreet about their mutual plans. Perhaps they tell an intimate or two, perhaps no one, but since they drive off to Provincetown on a whim, and in a rented car, the perpetrator need only—should the deed be done—drive their car one hundred and twenty miles back to Boston and leave it on the street. Assuming the bodies have been well-buried, it would be weeks, if ever, before any concern for the man and woman as missing persons might stir newspaper publicity in these parts. By then, would anyone at The Widow's Walk remember their faces? Even in that event, the police would have to assume, given the location of the car, that they returned to Boston and met their end there. I lived within the logic of this fine scenario, enjoyed my drink a little more, enjoyed the power I possessed over them by thinking thoughts such as these, and there . . . it is precisely there . . . I lost the rest of the evening. In the morning I would no longer be able to put it together to satisfy myself.

What I can't recollect is whether or not I began to drink again with Pond and Pangborn. It is as likely, I should think, that I boozed by myself, got into my car and went home. If I did, I would have gone directly to sleep. Although that, by the evidence of what I found when I awakened, was not possible.

I also have another scenario, which is certainly clearer than a dream, although I could have dreamt it. It is that Patty Lareine returned and we had a terrible quarrel. I see her mouth. Yet I do not recollect a word. Could it have been a dream?

Then I also have the clearest impression that Jessica and Leonard did indeed join me after they ate, and I invited them to my home (to Patty Lareine's home). We sat in the living room while the man and woman listened to me with attention. I seem to remember that. Then we took a trip in a car, but if it was my Porsche, I could not have taken both of them. Perhaps we went in two cars.

I also remember returning home alone. The dog was in terror of me. He is a big Labrador but he crept away as I came near. I sat down at the edge of my bed and jotted one more note before I lay down. That I recall. I dozed off sitting up and staring at the notebook. Then I woke up a few seconds (or was it an hour?) and read what I had written: "Despair is the emotion we feel at the death of beings within us."

That was my last thought before I went to sleep. Yet none of these scenarios, nor very little of them, can be true—because when I woke in the morning, I had a tattoo on my arm that had not been there before.

Jeremiah Digges

....

The Sea Witch of Billingsgate

I HAVE HEARD that it is witch-haunted, this ground on both sides of the town line as you enter Wellfleet from the south.

Although several witches have been mentioned as haunters of the place, investigation reveals only one with proper credentials—the Sea Witch of Billingsgate—but she has a number of exploits to her credit. They pop up through several centuries of local lore, suggesting almost as many lives for this creature as for her cat who was one of her ever-present "familiars."

Her main interest appears to have been in the marine phase of the business—contriving for the souls of lost sailors

Jeremiah Digges, the pen name of Joseph Berger, left New York City for Provincetown following the Crash of 1929. "The Sea Witch" is from a compilation called Cape Cod Pilot, written in 1937 as part of the Federal Writer's Project.

and such—but she had taken many a flyer among land-lubbers too. Wherever she may show, you can spot her by her heels. They were a weakness with her, those high red heels, and she affected them even at the risk of being frequently betrayed. Also, if business should ever take her abroad o' nights again, you will know her by her familiars running alongside—a cat and a gray goat with one glass eye.

Frankly, the chances are against meeting her. She has become inactive over these half-dozen decades just past. For one thing, business at sea has fallen off; and then, these Portuguese people have brought over effective counter-charms from the Old Country. We know now that if any witch should start cutting up didoes around our house, we can drive her away once and for all by sticking pins in the heart of a calf and dropping the heart down the chimney.

But the science of preventive conjury was unknown here in the heyday of the Sea Witch of Billingsgate. Some said she was a red girl, some said she was white. In her time, it is clear, she was both. Having heard something of the talents of these creatures, I would not begrudge her a Scot's plaid.

But her color or her form at a given time depended on the souls that was "betaken" by her at the moment. The notion that there was more than one witch operating in the territory is grossly unfair to the Lower Cape towns. It is a libel, an old wives' tale. And I should firmly refuse to believe anything—except, of course, that there was a Sea Witch of Billingsgate, and that her familiars were a cat and a gray goat with one glass eye.

Among the poor souls that were "betaken" was pretty little Goody Hallett of Eastham. Goody was only fifteen, and no more knowful of the black arts than a babe in swaddlecloth.

One spring night in 1715, Goody was seduced; and the following winter she was apprehended, lying in a barn, with a dead baby in her arms. She was at once whisked into the village, seized up to Deacon Doane's fine new whipping-post and given a lashing as a sort of preliminary to the real punishment that awaited the outcome of her trial for murder. Pending that, she was clapped into Eastham Gaol.

The poor girl asked only that she be allowed to die, and while the town fathers were inclined to oblige her in this, a little writhing first, they thought, might serve as a valuable warning to others of the godless younger generation of their day. The gaoler was cautioned against bringing Goody any victuals that wanted cutting with a knife.

One afternoon, while the girl was beating wildly against the bars of her cell window, a stranger sauntered up to the wall and stood looking in at her. He was dressed in fine French bombasset, and he carried a gold-tipped cane. Something about his gaze quieted Goody and kept her spellmoored. One of the iron cell bars stood between their faces. He reached out, took it lightly between his thumb and finger, and flicked it away—clean out of the window-frame—as if it were no more than a stray bit of ryestraw. Then he smiled and slowly shook his head.

"Ah, these stiff-necked hymn-bellerin' Yankees! I tell ye, sometimes they make me feel like the rawest greeny ever went on the account!"

The words meant nothing to little Goody Hallett, but in the man's voice there was something smooth and wisterly, something that tautened the spell.

"Now, my girl," he went on, flicking another bar out of the window, "I'm going to play ye fair and square, cross my—er, by yer leave. Ye're young, but ye've showed old enough, sartin, for the employment I can get ye. Ye can forget all this, child," and with a gesture, he tossed away still another bar from the window. "Yer life's still before ye. 'Tis all in the future—yes, hmmm!"

Soothingly, softly, he went on talking to her, but once he had led up to properly, he made no bones about who he was. And as he spoke, from time to time he punctuated his remarks by taking out the bars from the window, until all were gone, and Goody Hallett's way to freedom lay clear. Also, the while he spoke, the girl felt bitter against those who had not let her die; and beguiled into vengeful thoughts, she listened and nodded.

At last he took a paper from his waistcoat.

"Can you write, Goody? Well, no matter. A mark's as good. Just put it there, where the line's broken into small grains." He touched a gold quill to his tongue, and as Goody took the quill, she observed that the tip glistened scarlet. She was about to make the mark when he caught her arm.

"What! Tricks, is it? So soon?" His eyes were suddenly like fiery drills, and his fingers bruised her. But after a moment, he smiled again. "Young, aye! I forget ye're but a child, Goody Hallett. Go on and make yer mark; but if it's to be two lines, ye'll oblige me to make 'em slantindicular, like an X—not any other way."

Goody understood. And that night she disappeared from Eastham Gaol, and before her case could come up in General Court, the town of Eastham found that locks and bars could not hold Goody Hallett. No one seems to have thought of using silver "darbies" on her wrists—which would have done the trick—or else no one in Eastham was willing to give Deacon Doane's gaoler the loan of the silver. At any rate, Goody was finally "warned out" of Eastham town; and so she crossed into Billingsgate, where she lived in a lorn hut on the poverty-grass meadow, and where etarnal-strange capers were cut each night before cockcrow.

It is said that she took up quarters in a whale, and that she went cruising about, with a ship's light hung to the creature's tail, luring unwary mariners on the shoals. She dealt also in tempests, dabbled a bit in hurricanes, and now and then singled out some skipper who caught her fancy, to take him out at night, whisk him from the deck of his ship, bridle him and ride him up and down Cape Cod, and then send him back before morning, worn and creak-tinted from the cruel exertions. Now and then she selected a strong, good-looking young fo'mast hand for other kinds of "divarsion." For Goody, in her later years, had become a deep-dyed sinner, whom you would never have taken for the blossoming maid, once the pride of the hymn-singing Halletts of Eastham town.

Now, it has been said that the man who ruined Goody on that moonlit occasion under an old apple tree in 1715 was Black Bellamy himself. But I suspect that the tale grew of the fact that the pirate happened to be in Eastham in that year, and was wrecked two years later in the waters hard by. I have no doubt that Goody had a hand in brewing the April hurricane that brought on disaster to Bellamy's ship, the *Whidah*. But if she did, she was merely cooperating with her employer as she had done in a long string of other shipwrecks in the territory.

As the record shows, Sam Bellamy was a simple, blustering windbag of a fellow, and a furriner at that;

and I doubt if he was capable of the uncommon finesse it wanted, to trick the prettiest girl in a Cape Cod town. It wants a mite of doing to win one of these creatures, and in the version which I have heard of Goody's first fall, it seems to me the native touch was present.

The last official appearance of the Sea Witch of Billingsgate was as an Indian, living in the north end of town. On the record she is set down as Delilah Roach, and Delilah is described by the historians as the "sole survivor of the tribe of Nausets."

Well, Delilah herself insisted on having it that way. When the suspicion got around town that she was the Sea Witch, she marched right into the town clerk's office, to straighten the thing out—the way she wanted it straightened. And the town clerk, though he knew very well that Delilah's late husband, Simon Roach, had been the last *real* Indian, was not the man to cross Delilah. Her black eyes burned with the Unholy Powers as she stood over his table and commanded him to write, and as she commanded, so it was written. Delilah Roach was set down as the "last Indian." And as she flounced out of the office, the town clerk stole a glance at her. Beneath the hem of her skirt, which just missed sweeping the floor, his eye caught a brief spot of scarlet, now on the left side, now on the right.

Other townsfolk, even to the selectmen themselves, knew the importance of avoiding a "black conjury"; and in 1802, it was voted in town meeting "to repair the Indian's house and make her comfortable."

You will pass the spot where Delilah lies buried—or so we all hope—and I shall call it out to you, but by your leave, I shall describe it as the grave of the last Indian of Wellfleet.

Meanwhile, if you turn east from the highway at an intersection near the South Wellfleet depot, a dirt road will lead you through Goody Hallett's nocturnal stamping ground, to the sea.

Here it was, on the shoals a few hundred yards offshore, that Bellamy went aground in the *Whidah*. When she capsized, broke up, and left the bodies of 101 buccaneers alongshore for Captain Cyprian Southack to bury, she carried in her strong-chests such cash on hand as Sam had come by in a short but lively career. Captain Southack duly found the dead, but not the money, which is said to have been in gold coins, filling a great iron pot. It may still be in the neighborhood; it may be scattered to brighten the abode of the groundfish just beyond the low tidemark; it may have been taken off by the mooncussers, or it may have been recovered by those two red-coated strangers who came in the night to Gull Pond with pick and chart, and who then were seen no more.

John Cheever

The Chaste Clarissa

THE EVENING BOAT for Vineyard Haven was loading freight.
In a little while, the warning whistle would separate the sheep
from the goats—that's the way Baxter thought of it—the
islanders from the tourists wandering through the streets of
Woods Hole. His car, like all the others ticketed for the ferry,
was parked near the wharf. He sat on the front bumper,
smoking. The noise and movement of the small port seemed
to signify that the spring had ended and that the shores of
West Chop, across the Sound, were the shores of summer, but

Novelist and short-story writer John Cheever won the 1979 Pulitzer Prize for
The Stories of John Cheever. His career was built upon amusing, ironic
depictions of the affluent inhabitants of New York, New England and, in this case,
Martha's Vineyard.

the implications of the hour and the voyage made no impression on Baxter at all. The delay bored and irritated him. When someone called his name, he got to his feet with relief.

It was old Mrs. Ryan. She called to him from a dusty station wagon, and he went over to speak to her. "I knew it," she said. "I knew that I'd see someone here from Holly Cove. I had that feeling in my bones. We've been traveling since nine this morning. We had trouble with the brakes outside Worcester. Now I'm wondering if Mrs. Talbot will have cleaned the house. She wanted seventy-five dollars for opening it last summer and I told her I wouldn't pay her that again, and I wouldn't be surprised if she's thrown all my letters away. Oh, I hate to have a journey end in a dirty house, but if worse comes to worst, we can clean it ourselves. Can't we, Clarissa?" she asked, turning to a young woman who sat beside her on the front seat. "Oh, excuse me, Baxter!" she exclaimed. "You haven't met Clarissa, have you? This is Bob's wife, Clarissa Ryan."

Baxter's first thought was that a girl like that shouldn't have to ride in a dusty station wagon; she should have done much better. She was young. He guessed that she was about twenty-five. Red-headed, deep-breasted, slender, and indolent, she seemed to belong to a different species from old Mrs. Ryan and her large-boned, forthright daughters. "'The Cape Cod girls, they have no combs. They comb their hair with codfish bones,'" he said to himself but Clarissa's hair was well groomed. Her bare arms were perfectly white. Woods Hole and the activity on the wharf seemed to bore her and she was not interested in Mrs. Ryan's insular gossip. She lighted a cigarette.

At a pause in the old lady's monologue, Baxter spoke to her daughter-in-law. "When is Bob coming down, Mrs. Ryan?" he asked.

"He isn't coming at all," the beautiful Clarissa said. "He's in France. He's—"

"He's gone there for the government," old Mrs. Ryan interrupted, as if her daughter-in-law could not be entrusted with this simple explanation. "He's working on this terribly interesting project. He won't be back until autumn. I'm going abroad myself. I'm leaving Clarissa alone. Of course," she added forcefully, "I expect that she will *love* the island. Everyone does. I expect that she will be kept very busy. I expect that she—"

The warning signal from the ferry cut her off. Baxter said goodbye. One by one, the cars drove aboard, and the boat started to cross the shoal water from the mainland to the resort. Baxter drank a beer in the cabin and watched Clarissa and old Mrs. Ryan, who were sitting on deck. Since he had never seen Clarissa before, he supposed that Bob Ryan must have married her during the past winter. He did not understand how this beauty had ended up with the Ryans. They were a family of passionate amateur geologists and bird-watchers. "We're all terribly keen about birds and rocks," they said when they were introduced to strangers. Their cottage was a couple of miles from any other and had, as Mrs. Ryan often said, "been thrown together out of a barn in 1922." They sailed, hiked, swam in the surf, and organized expeditions to Cuttyhunk and Tarpaulin Cove. They were people who emphasized *corpore sano* unduly, Baxter thought, and they shouldn't leave Clarissa alone in the cottage. The wind had blown a strand of her flame-colored hair across her cheek. Her long legs were crossed. As the ferry entered the harbor, she stood up and made her way down the deck against the light salt wind, and Baxter, who had returned to the island indifferently, felt that the summer had begun.

BAXTER KNEW THAT in trying to get some information about Clarissa Ryan he had to be careful. He was accepted in Holly Cove because he had summered there all his life. He could be pleasant and he was a good-looking man, but his two divorces, his promiscuity, his stinginess, and his Latin complexion had left with his neighbors a vague feeling that he was unsavory. He learned that Clarissa had married Bob Ryan in November and that she was from Chicago. He heard people say that she was beautiful and stupid. That was all he did find out about her.

He looked for Clarissa on the tennis courts and the beaches. He didn't see her. He went several times to the beach nearest the Ryans' cottage. She wasn't there. When he had been on the island only a short time, he received from Mrs. Ryan, in the mail, an invitation to tea. It was an invitation that he would not ordinarily have accepted, but he drove eagerly that afternoon over to the Ryans' cottage. He was late. The cars of most of his friends and neighbors were parked in Mrs. Ryan's field. Their voices drifted out of the open windows into the garden, where Mrs. Ryan's climbing roses were in bloom. "Welcome aboard!" Mrs. Ryan shouted when he crossed the porch. "This is my farewell party. I'm going to Norway." She led him into a crowded room.

Clarissa sat behind the teacups. Against the wall at her back was a glass cabinet that held the Ryans' geological specimens. Her arms were bare. Baxter watched them while she poured his tea. "Hot? . . . Cold? Lemon? . . . Cream?" seemed to be all she had to say, but her red hair and her white arms dominated that end of the room. Baxter ate a sandwich. He hung around the table.

"Have you ever been to the island before, Clarissa?" he asked.

"Yes."

"Do you swim at the beach at Holly Cove?"

"It's too far away."

"When your mother-in-law leaves," Baxter said, "you must let me drive you there in the mornings. I go down at eleven."

"Well, thank you." Clarissa lowered her green eyes. She seemed uncomfortable, and the thought that she might be susceptible crossed Baxter's mind exuberantly. "Well, thank you," she repeated, "but I have a car of my own and—well, I don't know, I don't—"

"What are you two talking about?" Mrs. Ryan asked, coming between them and smiling wildly in an effort to conceal some of the force of her interference. "I know it isn't geology," she went on, "and I know that it isn't birds, and I know that it can't be books or music, because those are all things that Clarissa doesn't like, aren't they, Clarissa? Come with me, Baxter," and she led him to the other side of the room and talked to him about sheep raising. When the conversation had ended the party itself was nearly over. Clarissa's chair was empty. She was not in the room. Stopping at the door to thank Mrs. Ryan and say goodbye, Baxter said that he hoped she wasn't leaving for Europe immediately.

"Oh, but I am," Mrs. Ryan said. "I'm going to the mainland on the six-o'clock boat and sailing from Boston at noon tomorrow."

At half past ten the next morning, Baxter drove up to the Ryans' cottage. Mrs. Talbot, the local woman who helped the Ryans with their housework, answered the door. She said that young Mrs. Ryan was home, and let him in. Clarissa came downstairs. She looked more beautiful than ever, although she seemed put out at finding him there. She accepted his invitation to go swimming, but she accepted it unenthusiastically. "Oh, all right," she said.

When she came downstairs again, she had on a bathrobe over her bathing suit, and a broad-brimmed hat. On the drive to Holly Cove, he asked about her plans for the summer. She was noncommittal. She seemed preoccupied and unwilling to talk. They parked the car and walked side by side over the dunes to the beach, where she lay in the sand with her eyes closed. A few of Baxter's friends and neighbors stopped to pass the time, but they didn't stop for long, Baxter noticed. Clarissa's unresponsiveness made it difficult to talk. He didn't care.

He went swimming. Clarissa remained on the sand, bundled in her wrap. When he came out of the water, he lay down near her. He watched his neighbors and their children. The weather had been fair. The women were tanned. They were all married women and, unlike Clarissa, women with children, but the rigors of marriage and childbirth had left them all pretty, agile, and contented. While he was admiring them, Clarissa stood up and took off her bathrobe.

Here was something else, and it took his breath away. Some of the inescapable power of her beauty lay in the whiteness of her skin, some of it in the fact that, unlike the other women, who were at ease in bathing suits, Clarissa seemed humiliated and ashamed to find herself wearing so little. She walked down toward the water as if she were naked. When she first felt the water, she stopped short, for, again unlike the others, who were sporting around the pier like seals, Clarissa didn't like the cold. Then, caught for a second between nakedness and the cold, Clarissa waded in and swam a few feet. She came out of the water, hastily wrapped herself in the robe, and lay down in the sand. Then she spoke, for the first time that morning—for the first time in Baxter's experience—with warmth and feeling.

"You know, those stones on the point have grown a lot since I was here last," she said.

"What?" Baxter said.

"Those stones on the point," Clarissa said. "They've grown a lot."

"Stones don't grow," Baxter said.

"Oh yes they do," Clarissa said. "Didn't you know that? Stones grow. There's a stone in Mother's rose garden that's grown a foot in the last few years."

"I didn't know that stones grew," Baxter said.

"Well, they do," Clarissa said. She yawned; she shut her eyes. She seemed to fall asleep. When she opened her eyes again, she asked Baxter the time.

"Twelve o'clock," he said.

"I have to go home," she said. "I'm expecting guests."

Baxter could not contest this. He drove her home. She was unresponsive on the ride, and when he asked her if he could drive her to the beach again, she said no. It was a hot, fair day and most of the doors on the island stood open, but when Clarissa said goodbye to Baxter, she closed the door in his face.

Baxter got Clarissa's mail and newspapers from the post office the next day, but when he called with them at the cottage, Mrs. Talbot said that Mrs. Ryan was busy. He went that week to two large parties that she might have attended, but she was not at either. On Saturday night, he went to a barn dance, and late in the evening—they were dancing "Lady of the Lake"—he noticed Clarissa, sitting against the wall.

She was a striking wallflower. She was much more beautiful than any other woman there, but her beauty seemed to have intimidated the men. Baxter dropped out of the dance when he could and went to her. She was sitting on a packing case. It was the first thing she complained about. "There isn't even anything to sit on," she said.

"Don't you want to dance?" Baxter asked.

"Oh, I love to dance," she said. "I could dance all night, but I don't think *that's* dancing." She winced at the music of the fiddle and the piano. "I came with the Hortons. They just told me there was going to be a dance. They didn't tell me it was going to be this kind of a dance. I don't like all that skipping and hopping."

"Have your guests left?" Baxter asked.

"What guests?" Clarissa said.

"You told me you were expecting guests on Tuesday. When we were at the beach."

"I didn't say they were coming on Tuesday, did I? Clarissa asked. "They're coming tomorrow."

"Can't I take you home?" Baxter asked.

"All right."

He brought the car around to the barn and turned on the radio. She got in and slammed the door with spirit. He raced the car over the back roads, and when he brought it up to the Ryans' cottage, he turned off the lights. He watched her hands. She folded them on her purse. "Well, thank you very much," she said. "I was having an awful time and you saved my life. I just don't understand this place, I guess. I've always had plenty of partners, but I sat on that hard box for nearly an hour and nobody even spoke to me. You saved my life."

"You're lovely, Clarissa," Baxter said.

"Well," Clarissa said, and she sighed. "That's just my outward self. Nobody knows the real me."

That was it, Baxter thought, and if he could only adjust his flattery to what she believed herself to be, her scruples would dissolve. Did she think of herself as an actress, he wondered, a Channel swimmer, an heiress? The intimations of susceptibility that came from her in the summer night were so powerful, so heady, that they convinced Baxter that here was a woman whose chastity hung by a thread.

"I think I know the real you," Baxter said.

"Oh no you don't," Clarissa said. "Nobody does."

The radio played some lovelorn music from a Boston hotel. By the calendar, it was still early in the summer, but it seemed, from the stillness and the hugeness of the dark trees, to be much later. Baxter put his arms around Clarissa and planted a kiss on her lips.

She pushed him away violently and reached for the door. "Oh, now you've spoiled everything," she said as she got out of the car. "Now you've spoiled everything. I know what you've been thinking. I know you've been thinking it all along." She slammed the door and spoke to him across the window. "Well, you needn't come around here any more, Baxter," she said. "My girl friends are coming down from New York tomorrow on the morning plane and I'll be too busy to see you for the rest of the summer. Good night."

BAXTER WAS AWARE that he had only himself to blame; he had moved too quickly. He knew better. He went to bed feeling angry and sad, and slept poorly. He was depressed when he woke, and his depression was deepened by the noise of a sea rain, blowing in from the northeast. He lay in bed listening to the rain and the surf. The storm would metamorphose the island. The beaches would be empty. Drawers would stick. Suddenly he got out of bed, went to the telephone, called the airport. The New York plane had been unable to land, they told him, and no more planes were expected that day. The storm seemed to be playing directly into his hands. At noon, he drove in to the village and bought a Sunday paper and a box of candy. The candy was for Clarissa, but he was in no hurry to give it to her.

She would have stocked the icebox, put out the towels, and planned the picnic, but now the arrival of her friends had been postponed, and the lively day that she had anticipated had turned out to be rainy and idle. There were ways, of course, for her to overcome her disappointment, but on the evidence of the barn dance he felt that she was lost without her husband or her mother-in-law, and that there were few, if any, people on the island who would pay her a chance call or ask her over for a drink. It was likely that she would spend the day listening to the radio and the rain and that by the end of it she would be ready to welcome anyone, including Baxter. But as long as the forces of loneliness and idleness were working on his side, it was shrewder, Baxter knew, to wait. It would be best to come just before dark, and he waited until then. He drove to the Ryans' with his box of candy. The windows were lighted. Clarissa opened the door.

"I wanted to welcome your friends to the island," Baxter said. "I—"

"They didn't come," Clarissa said. "The plane couldn't land. They went back to New York. They telephoned me. I had planned such a nice visit. Now everything's changed."

"I'm sorry, Clarissa," Baxter said. "I've brought you a present."

"Oh!" She took the box of candy. "What a beautiful box! What a lovely present! What—" Her face and her voice were, for a minute, ingenuous and yielding, and then he saw the force of resistance transform them. "You shouldn't have done it," she said.

"May I come in?" Baxter asked.

"Well, I don't know," she said. "You can't come in if you're just going to sit around."

"We could play cards," Baxter said.

"I don't know how," she said.

"I'll teach you," Baxter said.

"No," she said. "No, Baxter, you'll have to go. You just don't understand the kind of woman I am. I spent all day writing a letter to Bob. I wrote and told him that you kissed me last night. I can't let you come in." She closed the door.

From the look on Clarissa's face when he gave her the box of candy, Baxter judged that she liked to get presents. An inexpensive gold bracelet or even a bunch of flowers might do it, he knew, but Baxter was an extremely stingy man, and while he saw the usefulness of a present, he could not bring himself to buy one. He decided to wait.

The storm blew all Monday and Tuesday. It cleared on Tuesday night, and by Wednesday afternoon the tennis courts were dry and Baxter played. He played until late. Then, when he had bathed and changed his clothes, he stopped at a cocktail party to pick up a drink. Here one of his neighbors, a married woman with four children, sat down beside him and began a general discussion of the nature of married love.

It was a conversation, with its glances and innuendoes, that Baxter had been through many times, and he knew roughly what it promised. His neighbor was one of the pretty mothers that Baxter had admired on the beach. Her hair was brown. Her arms were thin and tanned. Her teeth were sound. But while he appeared to be deeply concerned with her opinions on love, the white image of Clarissa loomed up in his mind, and he broke off the conversation and left the party. He drove to the Ryans'.

From a distance, the cottage looked shut. The house and the garden were perfectly still. He knocked and then rang. Clarissa spoke to him from an upstairs window.

"Oh, hello, Baxter," she said.

"I've come to say goodbye, Clarissa," Baxter said. He couldn't think of anything better.

"Oh, dear," Clarissa said. "Well, wait just a minute, I'll be down."

"I'm going away, Clarissa," Baxter said when she opened the door. "I've come to say goodbye."

"Where are you going?"

"I don't know." He said this sadly.

"Well, come in, then," she said hesitantly. "Come in for a minute. This is the last time that I'll see you, I guess, isn't it? Please excuse the way the place looks. Mr. Talbot got sick on Monday and Mrs. Talbot had to take him to the hospital on the mainland, and I haven't had anybody to help me. I've been all alone.

He followed her into the living room and sat down. She was more beautiful than ever. She talked about the problems that had been presented by Mrs. Talbot's departure. The fire in the stove that heated the water had died. There was a mouse in the kitchen. The bathtub wouldn't drain. She hadn't been able to get the car started.

In the quiet house, Baxter heard the sound of a leaky water tap and a clock pendulum. The sheet of glass that protected the Ryans' geological specimens reflected the fading sky outside the window. The cottage was near the water, and he could hear the surf. He noted these details dispassionately and for what they were worth. When Clarissa finished her remarks about Mrs. Talbot, he waited a full minute before he spoke.

"The sun is in your hair," he said.

"What?"

"The sun is in your hair. It's a beautiful color."

"Well, it isn't as pretty as it used to be," she said. "Hair like mine gets dark. But I'm not going to dye it. I don't think that women should dye their hair."

"You're so intelligent," he murmured.

"You don't mean that?"

"Mean what?"

"Mean that I'm intelligent."

"Oh, but I do," he said. "You're intelligent. You're beautiful. I'll never forget that night I met you at the boat. I hadn't wanted to come to the island. I'd made plans to go out West."

"I can't be intelligent," Clarissa said miserably. "I must be stupid. Mother Ryan says that I'm stupid, and Bob says that I'm stupid, and even Mrs. Talbot says that I'm stupid, and—" She began to cry. She went to a mirror and dried her eyes. Baxter followed. He put his arms around her. "Don't put your arms around me," she said, more in despair than in anger. "Nobody ever takes me seriously until they get their arms around me." She sat down again and Baxter sat near her. "But you're not stupid, Clarissa," he said. "You have a wonderful intelligence, a wonderful mind. I've often thought so. I've often felt that you must have a lot of very interesting opinions."

"Well, that's funny," she said, "because I do have a lot of opinions. Of course, I never dare say them to anyone, and Bob and Mother Ryan don't ever let me speak. They always interrupt me, as if they were ashamed of me. But I do have these opinions. I mean, I think we're like cogs in a wheel. I've concluded that we're like cogs in a wheel. Do you think we're like cogs in a wheel?"

"Oh, yes," he said. "Oh, yes, I do!"

"I think we're like cogs in a wheel," she said. "For instance, do you think that women should work? I've given that a lot of thought. My opinion is that I don't think married women should work. I mean, unless they have a lot of money, of course, but even then I think it's a full-time job to take care of a man. Or do you think that women should work?"

"What do you think?" he asked. "I'm terribly interested in knowing what you think."

"Well, my opinion is," she said timidly, "that

you just have to hoe your row. I don't think that working or joining the church is going to change everything, or special diets, either. I don't put much stock in fancy diets. We have a friend who eats a quarter of a pound of meat at every meal. He has a scales right at the table and he weighs the meat. It makes the table look awful and I don't see what good it's going to do him. I buy what's reasonable. If ham is reasonable, I buy ham. If lamb is reasonable, I buy lamb. Don't you think that's intelligent?"

"I think that's very intelligent."

"And progressive education," she said. "I don't have a good opinion of progressive education. When we go to the Howards' for dinner, the children ride their tricycles around the table all the time, and it's my opinion that they get this way from progressive schools, and that children ought to be told what's nice and what isn't."

The sun that had lighted her hair was gone, but there was still enough light in the room for Baxter to see that as she aired her opinions, her face suffused with color and her pupils dilated. Baxter listened patiently, for he knew by then that she merely wanted to be taken for something she was not—that the poor girl was lost. "You're very intelligent," he said, now and then. "You're so intelligent."

It was as simple as that.

Mary Oliver

....

Mussels

IN THE RIPRAP,
       in the cool caves,
              in the dim and salt-refreshed
                  recesses, they cling
in dark clusters,
       in barnacled fistfuls,
              in the dampness that never
                  leaves, in the deeps
of high tide, in the slow
       washing away of the water

Mary Oliver has garnered numerous literary awards for her poetry, including the 1984 Pulitzer Prize for American Primitive. Born in Ohio in 1935, Oliver has lived in Provincetown since 1964.

in which they feed,

in which the blue shells

open a little, and the orange bodies

make a sound

not loud,

not unmusical, as they take

nourishment, as the ocean

enters their bodies. At low tide

I am on the riprap, clattering

with boots and a pail,

rock over rock; I choose

the crevice, I reach

forward into the dampness,

my hands feeling everywhere

for the best, the biggest. Even before

I decide which to take,

which to twist from the wet rocks,

which to devour,

they, who have no eyes to see with,

see me, like a shadow,

bending forward. Together

they make a sound,

not loud,

not unmusical, as they lean

into the rocks, away

from my grasping fingers.

Denis Johnson

....

Resuscitation of a Hanged Man

HE CAME THERE in the off-season. So much was off. All bets were off. The last deal was off. His timing was off, or he wouldn't have come here at this moment, and also every second arc lamp along the peninsular highway was switched off. He'd been through several states along the turnpikes, through weary tollgates and stained mechanical restaurants, and by now he felt as if he'd crossed a hostile foreign land to reach this fog with nobody in it, only yellow lights blinking and yellow signs wandering past the car's windows silently. There was a single fair-sized town on the peninsula,

---

This selection from Denis Johnson's fourth novel finds Leonard English escaping to off-season Cape Cod, hoping for a fresh start after a failed suicide attempt. Johnson is also the author of Angels, Fiskadoro, *and* The Stars at Noon.

a place with more than one shopping center in it and boarded-up seafood stands strung along the roadside, and the traveller, whose name was Leonard English, thought he'd stop there for a drink, just one drink, before going on. But he was drawn into a very interesting conversation with a man whose face got to look more and more like a dead pig's face in the dim red light. What they were talking about really wasn't all that memorable—it was more the man's face—but the drinks got slippery and English's money was all wet by the time he got out of there, and as he made a U-turn through an intersection the world seemed to buckle beneath him and the car's hood flew up before the window. English held the wheel and jammed the brake, waiting for the rest of this earthquake, or this bombing or God's wrath, to destroy the town. A shriek, like the tearing of metal train wheels along metal rails, died away. Somebody was opening the door for him . . . but he was opening the door for himself, and now he was getting out of the car. There wasn't any cataclysm. It was just a town at night, quiet and useless, with buildings that looked like big toys or false fronts lit by arc lamps and backed by tremendous bleakness. Somehow his Volkswagen had climbed up onto a traffic island. The whole thing would have been embarrassing, but he couldn't seem to form any clear picture of what had happened. Blood ran down his forehead and blinded half his sight. The air reeked: the tank was ripped and twenty dollars' worth of gasoline covered the asphalt. In his imagination it burst into flames. A cabdriver stopped and came to stand beside him and said, "You made a wrong turn." English did not dispute this.

TO REACH HIS destination at the end of the Cape, English engaged the cabdriver's services, services he couldn't afford any more than he was going to be able to afford this accident.

"He gonna chadge you exry," the cabdriver said.

Chadge? English guessed the driver was talking about the old man who'd towed his car away, but what was he trying to say? "Right," English said.

"You from Bwostin?" the cabbie asked him.

This was just what the policeman had asked him amid the wreckage, saying *Boston* like *Bwostin.* "Mr. Leonard English," the officer had said. Looking right at English's Midwestern driver's license, he had inquired after his origins: "You from Bwostin?" "I just got here from Lawrence, Kansas," English told the officer. "*Kansas?*" the officer said. "Lawrence, Kansas?"—and English said yes. A little later the officer said, "You're drunk. But I'm gonna let you off."

"Drunk? I'm not drunk," English said.

"Yes you are, you most definitely are," the officer said, "or you wou'nt be arguing with me." With a certain vague tenderness, he was applying a Band-Aid to English's forehead.

English said, "I'm a little tipsy. I don't understand what you're saying."

"That's better," the officer said.

English was glad when the policeman left him in the cabdriver's custody, because he felt cut off from the world here, and to be scrutinized by a powerful figure in a place he hadn't even seen in the daylight yet left him shaken. Properly speaking, this wasn't even a peninsula. He'd had to cross a large bridge to get here. It was an island. A place apart.

And now, as they rattled toward this phony peninsula's other end, English was sitting up front with the cabdriver. English was dizzy, and on top of that there seemed to be an exhaust leak, but the driver kept saying, "You're A-OK now, brother." "No, I'm not," English said. They weren't in a taxicab. It was almost six in the morning and the driver was going in his station wagon to his home a couple of towns down the road, taking English dozens of miles out of his way for twenty dollars. "I like to drive," the cabbie said. He puffed on a joint wrapped in yellow paper.

English turned it down. "Grass makes me feel kind of paranoid."

"I don't get paranoid," the driver said. But he was a paranoid personality if English had ever seen one. "This beyond here, this is absolutely black," the driver said, pointing with the glowing end of his reefer ahead, to where the four-lane highway turned two-way. "No more lights, no more houses"—he drew a chestful of smoke—"nuthin, nuthin, nuthin. We won't see no traffic. Not car one." Immediately the red taillights of another car shone ahead. "I think I know this guy." He stomped the gas. "I think this is Danny Moss"—pronounced Dyany Mwas—"is that a Toyota? Cheez, looka how fast this guy's running." They were doing eighty. "*We're* gonna catch you, Danny. *We're* gaining on this sucker." But they were falling behind. "Ain't that a Toyota?" he said. The red taillights ahead went right, and the cabdriver's gaze followed their course as he and his passenger sailed past the turn they'd taken. "Yeah, that's a Toyota! Yeah, that's him! Yeah, that's Danny Moss!"

Actually they hadn't come to any place of absolute blackness. In a little while the sun was up, burning without heat above the road, and before they reached Provincetown they sped through three or four more little villages, in one of which they stopped and had breakfast. It turned out that Phil, the driver, sub-scribed to the branch of historical thought characterized by a belief in extraterrestrial interference, previous highly advanced civilizations, and future global cata-clysms, both human-made and geological. English now learned something about these things. "All the elemental phosphorus is gonna be like zero, completely gone. We'll be strangling each other in the streets for a little phosphorus," Phil said, "elemental phosphorus. The roads are gonna run with blood. Nobody even knows about it. Nobody's even surprised. Five thousand years ago on the earth they had a big cataclysm and a huge, what is it, whatyoucallit, megadeath. Partly because of running out of some of these elements you need in your body, like phosphorus." He got into a philosophical talk with their waitress and told her, "I think our world could really be some form of Hell, you know what I'm saying?" The waitress saw his point. "There's so much suffering here on earth," she said. Phil knew all the waitresses, and it was after nine when they got back on the road.

English fell asleep. When he woke up, the route had gone strange. White dunes made walls on either side of them. European music came out of the radio. They drove through a drift of sand.

In a few minutes his head was clear again, and he was looking at the sandy outskirts of the last town in America. The sun was shining above it now. A tower made of stone rose up in the distance. The seaside curved north, to their left, and the wooden buildings were laid out solid, bright and still as a painting, against the beach.

They followed the road into town and lost sight
of the harbor as they came down the main street of
shops. Now there were pedestrians moving alongside
them in the chilly sunshine. The traffic crawled. "This
crowd is nothing compared to summer," Phil told him.
Half the shops appeared closed, and English had a sense
of people walking around here where they didn't belong,
in an area that might have been abandoned after a panic.
Three ungainly women—were they men, in bright
skirts?—danced a parody of a chorus line by a tavern's
door, arms around one another's shoulders. Passing
along the walks and ambling down the middle of the
street were people in Bermuda shorts and children eating
ice-cream cones as if it weren't under 60 Fahrenheit
today. On the lawn of the town hall, surrounded by grey
pigeons and scattering crusts of bread out of a white
paper bag, stood a woman who was very clearly not a
woman but a man: as if a woman wore football shoulder
pads and other bulky protection beneath her very mod-
estly tailored dress. Another man in a dress was mailing
a letter at the blue mailbox just six feet away. And a
cross-dresser on roller skates loomed above two others
sitting on a bench, patting his brittle wig lightly with
one hand, the other hand on his hip, while laughter that
couldn't be heard passed among them. A very tall
woman, who might have been a man, talked with a
bunch of grade-school children out in front of a bakery.

English cleared his throat. He had a chance to look at everyone until he was sick of their faces, because the car wasn't getting anywhere.

Phil smacked the horn, but nothing happened. "Horn don't work. This is making me apeshit. I'm gonna run some bastards over."

They found the source of the traffic jam four blocks down, where a huge-bottomed transvestite comedian on the balcony of a cabaret-and-hotel delivered his Mae West impersonation for free. "Move over, honey!" he shouted down to a woman in a halted convertible. The woman ducked her head in embarrassment and put her hand on the arm of the man driving. Around them the shoppers and tourists, variously shocked and mesmerized, or curious and entertained, laughed at the comedian with his cascading platinum wig and his stupendous, unexplainable breasts. Later that night English would see someone being carried on a stretcher out of the side doors of this building and through the wet, falling snow to an ambulance. And he would think of this man on the balcony in his evening gown making jokes about his potbelly, gripping it with a hand that glittered with rings while flapping his huge false eyelashes, and English wouldn't feel equipped, he wouldn't feel grown-up enough, to be told the whole story about this town.

PHIL KNEW ANY number of people in Provincetown. He was connected all up and down the Cape. Long before the Pilgrims, English gathered, long before the Indians, way back past the time of cataclysms, even before the golden age of the extraterrestrial star-wanderers who had mated with monkeys to produce us all, members of Phil's family had arrived here and opened small dark restaurants with steamy walls and radios chattering and yowling in the kitchen, and had applied for liquor licenses which to this day they were denied because the grudges against them, though small ones, were eternal. What all this meant was that English wouldn't have to go to a motel. Phil had a cousin who ran a rooming house, freshly painted white and spilling winter roses over a knee-high picket fence, where English could stay cheaply.

Phil insisted on carrying English's suitcase up the long stairs through an atmosphere of mingled disinfectant and air-freshening spray into a room that was small but not cheerless. There were big orange ladybugs printed on the white curtains. A faintly discolored portrait of John F. Kennedy hung on the wall above the desk. The bathroom looked harmless—blue sink, blue toilet, blue tub scoured nearly white. "All right, hey, not bad," English assured Phil, but it had every quality of the end of the line.

Now that they'd travelled together and English was one of the family, with his very own room in

Phil's illustrious cousin's house, Phil wouldn't accept a fare. English had to follow him down the stairs and out to his half-disintegrated yellow station wagon, insisting. Then he accepted the twenty-dollar bill that English pressed on him, and gripped the new tenant's hand with his, the money caught between their palms. His eyes were moist. They were two of the same sort, men past thirty without a lot to recommend them; but this happened to English every day. He had a feeling they'd stay strangers.

After Phil was gone, English lay on the bed awhile, but he couldn't sleep because it was daytime and also a little too quiet. He wondered if everybody was at work. Then he remembered that it was Sunday. They'd passed a church, he and Phil, as they'd inched in Phil's vehicle down to the end of Commercial Street, the street of shops, and then in the other direction down Bradford, now his street, the street of his home. English hadn't really noticed, but he thought it might have been a Catholic church. He thought he would go to Mass.

In his first few hours on this dismal Cape, before he'd even seen the daylight here, he'd managed to smash his car and put himself in debt to a strange and probably larcenous auto body shop. The idea of a fresh start took on value and weight as he splashed water on his face and, lacking any kind of towel, dried it with the corner of his bedspread, uncovering in the process a bare mattress. If Mass hadn't started at ten, it would be starting soon, at eleven.

IT TOOK ENGLISH only a few minutes to walk there—St. Peter's, a Catholic institution. He hadn't missed the service. Under a sky the color of iron, people were lugging themselves like laundry toward the big doors of the church. A black arrow outlined in silver directed English toward a side door if he wanted to confess his sins.

In a small room next door to the administrative offices, he found a priest bidding goodbye to an old woman and cleaning his spectacles on the hem of his cassock. English backed away as she passed out of the place, and now it was his turn to sit in the wooden chair, separated from his confessor by a partition with little metal wheels.

This moment seemed to have swooped down on him from nowhere. He'd tried several times recently to make a good confession, but he'd failed. The problem was that about a year ago he'd more or less attempted to take his own life, to kill himself, and couldn't get started telling why.

The priest, a small, preoccupied man, made the sign of the cross and awaited the rote utterances, praying to himself in a rapid whisper.

But English had only one thing to confess. "I'm new in town—excuse me . . ." Violently he cleared his throat. Now he noticed the room was full of flowers.

The priest stopped praying. "Yes. Well, young friend. New in town."

"I wonder if—Father, can we dispense with the . . . ?" English waved his hand around, and was embarrassed to find that this gesture included the confessional and the cross. He'd meant only the formalities, the ritual. What he wanted was plain absolution.

"It's a nice quiet time of year to come," Father said in a puzzled tone.

English waited a minute. The flowers smelled terrible. "I just went crazy," he said. "I committed—I killed myself."

"Uh, you . . . " The priest looked up through the partition's screen as if only now beginning to see he wasn't by himself. "In what sense," he began, and didn't finish.

"What I mean is," English said, "not killed. Tried, I mean. I tried to hang myself."

"I see," Father said, meaning, perhaps, that he didn't see.

After a few seconds Father said, "Well then. You say you've tried to . . . Is there something you've done about this? Have you sought help?"

"I am. I'm—I'm confessing."

"But . . . " The priest stalled again.

English wondered how much time before Mass. Nobody else was behind him. "I mean . . . " he said.

"Okay," the priest said. "Go on."

"The thing is, I'm starting out here, starting over here." English had come too far. He wanted to find himself standing, without having moved, in the fresh air on the green lawn outside. It was December, but the lawns were still green. There were still flowers around town. He felt cut off from them and from all living things. "This suicide attempt is basically—that's the one thing I'm confessing," he said.

"Well then," Father said.

"I wanted to take Communion," English explained.

The priest seemed weighted down with sadness, but it might only have been shyness. "I don't sense much commitment," he said.

"Can't I just—"

"But I think, do you see, given your—lack—"

"I wanted to confess, I wanted to take Communion."

"Of course," Father said. "But—"

"I'll try again," English said. "I'll try later."

He left the place quickly, embarrassment crawling up his neck as he found his way to the door. Somehow he'd succeeded in confessing his greatest sin, yet had failed to find absolution. He felt hurt by this failure, really wounded. He couldn't hold himself up straight. It was hard for him to walk.

But his spirits lifted as he breathed the chilly air outside, where his fellow Christians ambled, most of them ignoring the paved walkway, across the lawn and through the church's double doors. He watched them awhile, and then, temporarily, he granted his own absolution. Self-absolution was allowed, he reasoned, in various emergencies. Wetting his fingers at the tiny front by the entrance and genuflecting once, he walked in among the aisles and pews with the touch of holy water drying on his forehead.

It was larger, more vaulting, than the church he'd gone to in Lawrence. At the front, behind the altar, the middle of the huge wall telescoped outward away from the congregation, making for the altar not just a great chamber that had nothing to do with the rest of the place but almost another world, because its three walls were given over completely to a gigantic mural depicting the wild ocean in a storm. In the middle of this storm a bigger-than-life-size Jesus stood on a black, sea-dashed rock in his milky garment. The amount of blue in this intimidating scene, sky blues and aquas and frothy blues and cobalts and indigos and azures, taking up about half of the congregation's sight, lent to their prayers a soft benedictive illumination like a public aquarium's. The wooden pews were as solid as concrete abutments on the highway, the whispers of those about to worship rocketed from wall to wall, and English's awareness of these things, along with his irritated awareness of the several babies in the place who would probably start their screams of torment soon, and all the boxes and slots for the seat donations and alms for the distant poor, and the long-handled baskets that would be poked under his nose, possibly more than once during the service, by two elderly men with small eyes whom he thought of against his will as God's goons, let him know that his attitude was all wrong today for church. But he was a Catholic. Having been here, he would forget all about it. But if he missed it, he would remember.

There were as many as fifty people scattered throughout a space that would have seated four hundred. All around him were persons he thought of as "Eastern," dark, European-looking persons. An attractive woman with black bangs and scarlet fingernails was sitting behind him, and English couldn't stop thinking about her all through the service. To get her legs out of his mind he swore to himself he'd talk to her on the way out and make her acquaintance. Then he started wondering if he would keep his promise, which wonder took him to the wonder of her legs again, and in this way he assembled himself to make a Holy Communion with his creator.

The tiny priest was a revolutionary: "I have been asked, the diocese has instructed us—all the parishes have received a letter that they are not to go out among the pews to pass the sign of peace." He seemed to get smaller and smaller. "But I'm going to have to just disregard that." A nervous murmuring in the congregation indicated they didn't know if they should applaud, or what. A couple of isolated claps served to express everyone's approval. " 'I give you peace; my peace I give you.' " Were they already at that part? The priest came among the pews and passed out a few handshakes, and the congregation all turned and shook hands with those nearest them.

It never seemed likely, it was never expected, but for English there sometimes came a moment, a time-out in the electric, a rushing movement of what he took to be his soul. "A death He freely accepted," the Silly Mister Nobody intoned, and raising up the wafer above the cup, he turned into a priest rising before Leonard English like the drowned, the robes dripping off him in the sun. Now English didn't have to quarrel, now he didn't have to ask why all these people expected to live forever. And then the feeling was gone. He'd lost it again. His mind wasn't focusing on anything. He'd had the best of intentions, but he was here in line for the wafer, the body of Christ burning purely out of time, standing up through two thousand years, not really here again . . . He was back on his knees in the pews with the body of Our Lord melting in his mouth, not really here again. Our Father, although I came here in faith, you gave me a brain where everything fizzes and nothing connects. I'll start meditating. I'm going to discipline my mind . . .

Everyone was standing up. It was over.

He went out the front way with the other pedestrians, not because he was one, although he was, but because he was trailing the woman who'd been sitting behind him. She was easy to keep in sight, but she walked fast.

She was halfway to the corner by the time he caught up. "My name's English," he told her.

"My name's Portuguese," she said.

"No, I mean, that's really my name, Lenny English." He couldn't get her to slow down. "What's your name?"

"Leanna."

"I was thinking we could have dinner, Leanna. I was thinking and hoping that."

"Not me," she said. "I'm strictly P-town."

"Strictly P-town. What does that mean?" he said.

"It means I'm gay." she said.

Had he been riding a bicycle, he'd have fallen off. He felt as if his startled expression must be ruining everything.

She walked on.

"Wait a minute, wait a minute," English said. "You don't look gay. Isn't that against the law? It'd be easier if you gave some indication."

She was amused, but not to the point of slowing down. "I must've been out of town when they passed out the little badges," she said.

"Couldn't we just have dinner anyway? I don't have anything against women who like women. I like women myself."

"I can't. I've got some other stuff to do." She smiled at him. "Do you know what?" she said. "You left your wallet in the church."

"My wallet?" He'd taken out his wallet to make a donation. Now it was gone from his pocket.

"It's sitting on the bench," she said. "I noticed when we all stood up."

"Oh, shit. Oh, great. How come you didn't tell me?"

"I just told you," Leanna said.

English wanted to talk more, but his anxiety was already carrying him back inside, against the tide of people flowing toward Bradford Street. He swiveled left and right, slipping through them sideways and apologizing convulsively, with an energy he'd lacked in the confessional: "Pardon me. Excuse me. Pardon me. Pardon me . . ."

Edgar Allan Poe

....

Narrative of Arthur Gordon Pym

My name is Arthur Gordon Pym. My father was a respectable trader in sea stores at Nantucket, where I was born. My maternal grandfather was an attorney in good practice. He was fortunate in everything, and had speculated very successfully in stocks of the Edgarton New-Bank, as it was formerly called. By these and other means he had managed to lay by a tolerable sum of money. He was more attached to myself, I believe, than to any other person in the world, and I expected to inherit the most of his property at his death. He sent me, at six years of age, to the school of old Mr. Ricketts,

---

Edgar Allan Poe's upbringing in the port cities of Richmond and Boston, his numerous coastal voyages, and his life-long fascination with science, laid the groundwork for the 1888 adventures of the Nantucket-based Arthur Gordon Pym.

a gentleman with only one arm, and of eccentric manners—he is well known to almost every person who has
visited New Bedford. I stayed at his school until I was
sixteen, when I left him for Mr. E. Ronald's academy on
the hill. Here I became intimate with the son of Mr.
Barnard, a sea captain, who generally sailed in the
employ of Lloyd and Vredenburgh—Mr. Barnard is also
very well known in New Bedford, and has many relations, I am certain, in Edgarton. His son was named
Augustus, and he was nearly two years older than
myself. He had been on a whaling voyage with his father
in the *John Donaldson*, and was always talking to me of his
adventures in the South Pacific Ocean. I used frequently
to go home with him, and remain all day, and sometimes all night. We occupied the same bed, and he
would be sure to keep me awake until almost light,
telling me stories of the natives of the Island of Tinian,
and other places he had visited in his travels. At last I
could not help being interested in what he said, and by
degrees I felt the greatest desire to go to sea. I owned a
sailboat called the *Ariel*, and worth about seventy-five
dollars. She had a half deck or cuddy, and was rigged
sloop-fashion—I forget her tonnage, but she would hold
ten persons without much crowding. In this boat we
were in the habit of going on some of the maddest
freaks in the world; and, when I now think of them, it
appears to me a thousand wonders that I am alive today.

I will relate one of these adventures by way of introduction to a longer and more momentous narrative. One night there was a party at Mr. Barnard's, and both Augustus and myself were not a little intoxicated towards the close of it. As usual, in such cases, I took part of his bed in preference to going home. He went to sleep, as I thought, very quietly (it being near one when the party broke up), and without saying a word on his favorite topic. It might have been half an hour from the time of our getting into bed, and I was just about falling into a doze, when he suddenly started up, and swore with a terrible oath that he would not go to sleep for any Arthur Pym in Christendom, when there was so glorious a breeze from the southwest. I never was so astonished in my life, not knowing what he intended, and thinking that the wines and liquors he had drunk had set him entirely beside himself. He proceeded to talk very coolly, however, saying he knew that I supposed him intoxicated, but that he was never more sober in his life. He was only tired, he added, of lying in bed on such a fine night like a dog, and was determined to get up and dress, and go out on a frolic with the boat. I can hardly tell what possessed me, but the words were no sooner out of his mouth than I felt a thrill of the greatest excitement and pleasure, and thought his mad idea one of the most delightful and most reasonable things in the world. It was blowing almost a gale, and the weather was very cold—it being late in October. I sprang out of bed, nevertheless, in a kind of ecstasy, and told him I was quite as brave as himself, and quite as tired as he was of lying in bed like a dog, and quite as ready for any fun or frolic as any Augustus Barnard in Nantucket.

We lost no time in getting on our clothes and hurrying down to the boat. She was lying at the old decayed wharf by the lumberyard of Pankey & Co., and almost thumping her sides out against the rough logs. Augustus got into her and bailed her, for she was nearly half full of water. This being done, we hoisted jib and mainsail, kept full, and started boldly out to sea.

The wind, as I before said, blew freshly from the southwest. The night was very clear and cold. Augustus had taken the helm and I stationed myself by the mast, on the deck of the cuddy. We flew along at a great rate—neither of us having said a word since casting loose from the wharf. I now asked my companion what course he intended to steer, and what time he thought it probable we should get back. He whistled for a few minutes, and then said crustily, "I am going to sea—you may go home if you think proper." Turning my eyes upon him, I perceived at once that, in spite of his assumed *nonchalance*, he was greatly agitated. I could see him distinctly by the light of the moon—his face was paler than any marble, and his hand shook so excessively that he could scarcely retain hold of the tiller. I found that something had gone wrong, and became seriously alarmed. At this period I knew little about the management of a boat, and was now depending entirely upon the nautical skill of my friend. The wind, too, had suddenly increased, and we were fast getting out of the lee of the land—still I was ashamed to betray any trepidation, and for almost half an hour maintained a resolute silence. I could stand it no longer, however, and spoke to Augustus about the propriety of turning back. As before, it was nearly a minute before he made answer, or took any notice of my suggestion. "By-and-by," said he at length—"time enough—home by-and-by." I had expected such a reply, but there was something in the tone of these words which filled me with an indescribable feeling of dread. I again looked at the speaker attentively. His lips were perfectly livid, and his knees shook so violently together that he seemed scarcely able to stand. "For God's sake, Augustus," I screamed, now heartily frightened, "what ails you?—what is the matter?—what *are* you going to do?" "Matter!" he stammered, in the greatest apparent surprise, letting go the tiller at the same moment, and falling forward into the bottom of the boat—"matter—why, nothing is the—matter—going home—d-d-don't you see?" The whole truth now flashed upon me. I flew to him and raised him up. He was drunk—beastly drunk—he could no longer either stand, speak, or see. His eyes were perfectly glazed; and as I let him go in the extremity of my despair, he rolled like a mere log into the bilge water from which I had lifted him. It was evident that, during the evening, he had drunk far more than I suspected, and that his conduct in bed had been the result of a highly concentrated state of intoxication—a state which, like madness, frequently enables the victim to imitate the outward demeanor of one in perfect possession of his senses. The coolness of the night air, however, had had its usual effect—the mental energy began to yield before its influence—and the confused perception which he no doubt then had of his perilous situation had assisted in hastening the catastrophe. He was now thoroughly insensible, and there was no probability that he would be otherwise for many hours.

It is hardly possible to conceive the extremity of my terror. The fumes of the wine lately taken had evaporated, leaving me doubly timid and irresolute. I knew that I was altogether incapable of managing the boat, and that a fierce wind and a strong ebb tide were hurrying us to destruction. A storm was evidently gathering behind us; we had neither compass nor provisions; and it was clear that, if we held our present course, we should be out of sight of land before daybreak. These thoughts, with a crowd of others equally fearful, flashed through my mind with a bewildering rapidity, and for some moments paralyzed me beyond the possibility of making any exertion. The boat was going through the water at a terrible rate—full before the wind—no reef in either jib or mainsail—running her bows completely under the foam. It was a thousand wonders she did not broach to—Augustus having let go the tiller, as I said before, and I being too much agitated to think of taking it myself. By good luck, however, she kept steady, and gradually I recovered some degree of presence of mind. Still the wind was increasingly fearfully; and whenever we rose from a plunge forward, the sea behind fell combing over our counter, and deluged us with water. I was so utterly benumbed, too, in every limb, as to be nearly unconscious of sensation. At length I summoned up the resolution of despair, and rushing to the mainsail, let it go by the run. As might have been expected, I flew over the bows, and, getting drenched with water, carried away the mast short off by the board. This latter accident alone saved me from instant destruction. Under the jib only, I now boomed along before the wind, shipping heavy seas occasionally over the counter, but relieved from the terror of immediate death. I took the helm and breathed with greater freedom, as I found that there yet remained to us a chance of ultimate escape. Augustus still lay senseless in the bottom of the boat; and as there was imminent danger of his drowning (the water being nearly a foot deep just where he fell), I contrived to raise him partially up, and keep him in a sitting position, by passing a rope round his waist, and lashing it to a ringbolt in the deck of the cuddy. Having thus arranged everything as well as I could in my chilled and agitated condition, I recommended myself to God, and made up my mind to bear whatever might happen with all the fortitude in my power.

Hardly had I come to this resolution when, suddenly, a loud and long scream or yell, as if from the throats of a thousand demons, seemed to pervade the whole atmosphere around and above the boat. Never while I live shall I forget the intense agony of terror I experienced at that moment. My hair stood erect on my head—I felt the blood congealing in my veins—my heart ceased utterly to beat, and without having once raised my eyes to learn the source of my alarm, I tumbled headlong and insensible upon the body of my fallen companion.

I found myself, upon reviving, in the cabin of a large whaling ship (the Penguin) bound to Nantucket. Several persons were standing over me, and Augustus, paler than death, was busily occupied in chafing my hands. Upon seeing me open my eyes, his exclamations of gratitude and joy excited alternate laughter and tears from the tough-looking personages who were present. The mystery of our being in existence was soon explained. We had been run down by the whaling-ship, which was close hauled, being up to Nantucket with every sail she could venture to set, and consequently running almost at right angles to our course. Several men were on the lookout forward, but did not perceive our boat until it was an impossibility to avoid coming in contact—their shouts of warning upon seeing us were what so terribly alarmed me. The huge ship, I was told, rode immediately over us with as much ease as our own little vessel would have passed over a feather, and without the least perceptible impediment to her progress. Not a scream arose from the deck of the victim—there was a slight grating sound to be heard mingling with the roar of the wind and water, as the frail bark which was swallow up rubbed for a moment along the keel of her destroyer—but this was all. Thinking our boat (which it will be remembered was dismasted) some mere shell cut adrift as useless, the captain (Captain E.T.V. Block of New London) was for proceeding on his course without troubling himself further about the matter. Luckily, there were two of the lookout who swore positively to having seen some person at our helm and represented the possibility of yet saving him. A discussion ensued, when Block grew angry, and, after awhile, said that "it was no business of his to be eternally watching for eggshells; that the ship should not put about for any such nonsense; and if there was a man run down, it was nobody's fault but his own—he might drown and be d—d," or some language to that effect. Henderson, the first mate, now took the matter up, being justly indignant, as well as the whole ship's crew, at a speech evincing so base a degree of heartless atrocity. He spoke plainly, seeing himself upheld by the men, told the captain he considered him a fit subject for the gallows, and that he would disobey his orders if he were hanged for it the moment he set his foot on shore. He strode aft, jostling Block (who turned very pale and made no answer) on one side, and seizing the helm, gave the word, in a firm voice, *Hard-a-lee!* The men flew to their posts, and the ship went cleverly about. All this had occupied nearly five minutes, and it was supposed to be hardly within the bounds of possibility that any individual could be saved—allowing any to have been on board the boat. Yet, as the reader has seen, both Augustus and myself were rescued; and our deliverance seems to have been brought about by two of those almost inconceivable pieces of good fortune which are attributed by the wise and pious to the special interference of Providence.

While the ship was yet in stays, the mate lowered the jolly boat and jumped into her with the very two men, I believe, who had spoke up as having seen me at the helm. They had just left the lee of the vessel (the moon still shining brightly) when she made a long and heavy roll to windward, and Henderson, at the same moment, starting up in his seat, bawled out to his crew to *back water.* He would say nothing else—repeating his cry impatiently, *back water! back water!* The men put back as speedily as possible; but by this time the ship had gone round, and gotten fully under headway, although all hands on board were making great exertions to take in sail. In despite of the danger of the attempt, the mate clung to the main-chains as soon as they came within his reach. Another huge lurch now brought the starboard side of the vessel out of water nearly as far as her keel, when the cause of his anxiety was rendered obvious enough. The body of a man was seen to be affixed in the most singular manner to the smooth and shining bottom (the *Penguin* was coppered and copper-fastened), and beating violently against it with every movement of the hull. After several ineffectual efforts, made during the lurches of the ship, and at the imminent risk of swamping the boat, I was finally disengaged from my perilous situation and taken on board—for the body proved to be my own. It appeared that one of the timber bolts having started and broken a passage through the copper, it had arrested my progress as I passed under the ship, and fastened me in so extraordinary a manner to her bottom. The head of the bolt had made its way through the collar of the green baize jacket I had on, and through the back port of my neck, forcing itself out between two sinews and just below the right ear. I was immediately put to bed—although life seemed to be totally extinct. There was no surgeon on board. The captain, however, treated me with every attention—to make amends, I presume, in the eyes of his crew, for his atrocious behavior in the previous portion of the adventure.

In the meantime, Henderson had again put off from the ship, although the wind was now blowing almost a hurricane. He had not been gone many minutes when he fell in with some fragments of our boat, and shortly afterward one of the men with his asserted that he could distinguish a cry for help at intervals amid the roaring of the tempest. This induced the hardy seamen to persevere in their search for more than a half an hour, although repeated signals to return were made them by Captain Block, and although every moment on the water in so frail a boat was fraught to them with the most imminent and deadly peril. Indeed, it is nearly impossible to conceive how the small jolly they were in could have escaped destruction for a single instant. She was built, however, for the whaling service, and was fitted, I have since had reason to believe, with air boxes, in the manner of some lifeboats used on the coast of Wales.

After searching in vain for about the period of time just mentioned, it was determined to get back to the ship. They had scarcely made this resolve when a feeble cry arose from a dark object that floated rapidly by. They pursued and soon overtook it. It proved to be the entire deck of the *Ariel*'s cuddy. Augustus was struggling near it, apparently in the last agonies. Upon getting hold of him it was found that he was attached by a rope to the floating timber. This rope, it will be remembered, I had myself tied round his waist, and made fast to a ringbolt, for the purpose of keeping him in an upright position, and my so doing, it appeared, had been ultimately the means of preserving his life. The *Ariel* was slightly put together, and in going down her frame naturally went to pieces; the deck of the cuddy, as might be expected, was lifted, by the force of the water rushing in, entirely from the main timbers, and floated (with other fragments, no doubt) to the surface—Augustus was buoyed up with it, and thus escaped a terrible death.

It was more than an hour after being taken on board the *Penguin* before he could give any account of himself, or be made to comprehend the nature of the accident which had befallen our boat. At length he became thoroughly aroused, and spoke much of his sensations while in the water. Upon his first attaining any degree of consciousness, he found himself beneath the surface, whirling round and round with inconceivable rapidity, and with a rope wrapped in three or four folds tightly about his neck. In an instant afterward he felt himself going rapidly upward, when, his head striking violently against a hard substance, he again relapsed into insensibility. Upon once more reviving he was in fuller possession of his reason—this was still, however, in the greatest degree clouded and confused. He now knew that some accident had occurred, and that he was in the water, although his mouth was above the surface, and he could breathe with some freedom. Possibly, at this period, the deck was drifting rapidly before the wind, and drawing him after it, as he floated upon his back. Of course, as long as he could have retained this position, it would have been nearly impossible that he should be drowned. Presently a surge threw him directly athwart the deck; and this post he endeavored to maintain, screaming at intervals for help. Just before he was discovered by Mr. Henderson, he had been obliged to relax his hold through exhaustion, and, falling into the sea, had given himself up for lost. During the whole period of his struggles he had not the faintest recollection of the *Ariel*, nor of any matters in connection with the source of his disaster. A vague feeling of terror and despair had taken entire possession of his faculties. When he was finally picked up, every power of his mind had failed him; and, as before said, it was nearly an hour after getting on board the *Penguin* before he became fully aware of his condition. In regard to myself—I was resuscitated from a state bordering very nearly upon death (and after every other means had been tried in vain for three hours and a half) by vigorous friction with flannels bathed in hot oil—a proceeding suggested by Augustus. The wound in my neck, although of an ugly appearance, proved of little real consequence, and I soon recovered from its effects.

The *Penguin* got into port about nine o'clock in the morning, after encountering one of the severest gales ever experienced off Nantucket. Both Augustus and myself managed to appear at Mr. Barnard's in time for breakfast—which, luckily, was somewhat late, owing to the party over night. I suppose all at the table were too much fatigued themselves to notice our jaded appearance—of course, it would not have borne a very rigid scrutiny. Schoolboys, however, can accomplish wonders in the way of deception, and I verily believe not one of our friends in Nantucket had the slightest suspicion that the terrible story told by some sailors in town of their having run down a vessel at sea and drowned some thirty or forty poor devils, had references either to the *Ariel*, my companion, or myself. We two have since very frequently talked the matter over—but never without a shudder. In one of our conversations Augustus frankly confessed to me, that in his whole life he had at no time experienced so excruciating a sense of dismay, as when on board our little boat he first discovered the extent of his intoxication, and felt himself sinking beneath its influence.

Helen Keller

A Summer in Brewster

JUST BEFORE THE Perkins Institution closed for the summer, it was arranged that my teacher and I should spend our vacation at Brewster, on Cape Cod, with our dear friend, Mrs. Hopkins. I was delighted, for my mind was full of the prospective joys and of the wonderful stories I had heard about the sea.

My most vivid recollection of that summer is the ocean. I had always lived far inland and had never had so much as a whiff of salt air; but I had read in a big book

---

Although Helen Keller became deaf and blind at an early age, through perseverance (with the assistance of Anne Sullivan of the Perkins Institution) Keller was able to leave a lasting contribution to social reform. This Cape reminiscence is from her autobiography.

called "Our World" a description of the ocean which filled me with wonder and an intense longing to touch the mighty sea and feel it roar. So my little heart leaped high with eager excitement when I knew that my wish was at last to be realized.

No sooner had I been helped into my bathing-suit than I sprang out upon the warm sand and without thought of fear plunged into the cold water. I felt the great billows rock and sink. The buoyant motion of the water filled me with an exquisite, quivering joy. Suddenly my ecstasy gave place to terror; for my foot struck against a rock and the next instant there was a rush of water over my head. I thrust out my hands to grasp some support, I clutched at the water and at the seaweed which the waves tossed in my face. But all my frantic efforts were in vain. The waves seemed to be playing a game with me, and tossed me from one to another in their wild frolic. It was fearful! The good, firm earth had slipped from my feet, and everything seemed shut out from this strange all-enveloping element— life, air, warmth and love. At last, however, the sea, as if weary of its new toy, threw me back on the shore, and in another instant I was clasped in my teacher's arms. Oh, the comfort of the long, tender embrace! As soon as I had recovered from my panic sufficiently to say anything, I demanded, "Who put salt in the water?"

Arturo Vivante

....

The Last Kiss

THE THEATER, A small and fragile building on a wharf, is
no more, burned down, set on fire by two local kids for kicks
one winter night, and, despite much fund raising, it has never
been rebuilt. Gone with it are the letters from Eugene O'Neill,
Tennessee Williams, and others that Julia Westcott had
received and framed, gone their photographs and the posters
of their plays that she had hung in the theater's lobby. She
had played in these and in a hundred others, but that was in
the past, long before Livio met her.

The Provincetown Players, including Eugene O'Neill, Tennessee Williams, and
Edna St. Vincent Millay, greatly influenced the Cape literary scene. In this story,
Arturo Vivante, a frequent contributor to The New Yorker, investigates the
famous theater.

By that time she was in her seventies and acting was behind her. She had withdrawn backstage, to support the new actors with her enthusiasm and what was left of her resources. The theater didn't belong to her, though once she'd had a share in it. In a way, though, it was more hers than anyone else's. She tended and preserved it till the flames turned it into ashes.

So it, too, like the plays it housed, had a dramatic ending, one more frightening and more real than any playwright or actor would dare to have staged. Now the sea breezes fan the vacant lot.

BUT ON AN early September weekend twenty years ago it stood there on the wharf intact, its weathered shingles as silver as the breaking waves, its door waiting to be opened, its curtain to be raised.

The play, which Livio had written, and which was almost as ephemeral as a day lily—it ran for just three nights—was entitled *Live Well*, the words Eskimos greet each other with in meeting and in parting. It had to do with their extreme hospitality to strangers, especially those who have lost their way and are dying of cold. It was really a very secondary play, but Livio believed in it perhaps more than he should have, and was in a pathetic state of expectation, tension, and excitement. He had quite fallen for the young actress— the wife, the provider of the warmth; he admired the

boy who played the stranger: and, though Livio would
have spoken the lines quite differently, he was very for-
giving of the actor who played the unjealous husband.
He was good friends with the director, and felt great
warmth for the spectators as they began streaming in and
filling the theater till there wasn't a vacant chair left. He
loved the town. He loved, in short, everyone, but most
of all Julia, the factotum, the animator, the spirit of the
place. The play itself could have been more subtle. Some
of the spectators, while keenly interested at first, disap-
proved of it as it went on, or so it seemed to him. It was
successful enough, though, for the company to feel quite
festive at the end, especially on the third and last night.

After that performance, Livio invited Julia, the
actors, the director, and other friends to a party at his
house, fourteen miles away. The weather all that weekend was so good that you couldn't feel sad summer was
coming to an end—the leaves, some already hemmed
gold or crimson, shone out; the horizon was so clear
that, in the daytime, you could see the outline of land
forty miles across the bay, and, at night its lights glitter-
ing. He drove alone with Julia in his old convertible.
They had known each other for two years now, and she
had put on two one-act plays of his the year before.
They had met at a party given by a friend—Sheila—at a
house not very far from his own. Julia and Livio had
talked about Chekhov and especially about Keats (her

favorite poet), and he felt almost as if Keats, and not Sheila, had introduced them. Julia had a graceful, frail, ethereal look about her, a poetic quality. When she told him she was past acting, he said, "But not playing," and they both laughed. Though married and in his mid-forties there was a certain innocence about him. He had a trusting smile, could not dissemble and was quite unpretentious. Beauty he could not ignore. Perhaps these traits endeared him to her. She might also have been attracted by his being Italian—she had studied the language, been to Italy, and as a young woman, in Boston, during the Sacco and Vanzetti trial, she had been arrested and spent a night in jail for demonstrating in their favor.

Tonight they drove not along the highway but along a winding back road. The top was down, the sky starry, the air balmy, the moon full. It was so beautiful he went very slowly. The crickets made a portentous din. "Between crickets and stars," she said. The whole night seemed to be singing. The low ground cover of bearberry, hayberry and beach plum gave them a wide view of the low hills and dunes bathed in moonlight. In the moon's delicate light, the ridges blended into each other softly, wave after wave, cast toward the ocean, west toward the bay, whose pearly ripple could here and there be seen. Then, in a valley, by a stream, the road went through a tall wood. Tall trees arched over the road, which became like a living tunnel. The sound of the motor and of the tires' tread mingled with the sound of the crickets. On a straight stretch of road, he stopped the car and switched off the engine. There was hardly any late traffic on the small road, and he put the lights out. The night seemed even more magical, and more tuneful. They turned to each other, and he took her up in his arms and he kissed her with passion. It was an ageless kiss—one in which age was forgotten, one in which they forgot themselves. Then they drove on. In his home at the party, again and again their eyes met, knowingly, rekindling the warmth of the kiss again and again in the fondest reflection.

His wife was there, but wasn't his play about free love? If it had a point at all, then it was that, the idea of no jealousy, of a love "that to divide is not to take away."

WINTERS JULIA SPENT not in the little town by the sea where the theater was, but in the city, in the first-floor apartment of a nice old red-brick building she owned on a pretty street. Sometimes he went to see her there purely for the pleasure of her company, to be in the presence of the grace of an earlier generation. Charity had nothing to do with his visits, rather they were like a bee's descent to a flower, which may do the flower some good, though doing good isn't the bee's intention. And they corresponded. Her letters were written in a flowing, clear, but not *too* clear hand, with some crossed-out words, as he thought letters should be written.

WITH THE PASSING of the years—she was now in her eighties—she rarely went out of her apartment. Though she could still read (and without glasses), her eyesight had weakened, so a friend had the idea of giving her a TV and asked others for contributions. Soon, enough money was collected for a large color set.

"Something is making everything much dimmer," she wrote Livio about the TV. Like city lights dimming the stars, he thought. Reading the letter, he could see her—an actress who had never had television, not because she couldn't afford it but because she regarded it as a brash and buzzing upstart that had put out the lights in many theaters, and silenced voices that were to her much dearer. Not to seem ungracious, she accepted the TV. And so, her letter continued, she would "try to like it for the sake of so many friends who insisted there were plays and wild animals to enjoy and talk about with them."

Giving her the set had certainly been a kind thing to do, and one could see why her friends thought she would appreciate the gift. Yet its introduction into her house seemed like a bad fifth act to a well wrought play. Less a gift than an unwitting corruption. It might help her pass the days and nights. She might become accustomed, even addicted to it, and miss it if it broke or was stolen. But it was sad, a little like bringing "the comforts of religion" to a dying heretic. Let people live and die according to their principles, Livio thought, and hadn't sent any money. He took her out to dinner and a play instead, taking great care to help her get down her doorstep and into his car which he had double-parked. They had dinner in a cozy little restaurant under candlelight. She looked at the white table cloth on which the wine cast red reflections. "Isn't it nice that these aren't stains," she said. "For a moment I thought I'd spilled some wine. Just scarlet lights."

The goblets were small, mere thimblefuls, but she got quite heady, and Livio had to hold her close as they climbed the marble staircase of the theater. Even so she almost stumbled. He held her closer still, his arm around her waist, and felt her warmth. After the play, taking her home, she found, to her delight, piled in a trash bin and sticking up like flowers, some gilded and quite unusual wooden decorations from an old house that was being remodeled, and she picked out a couple of them and carried them to her apartment, as joyful as could be. Perhaps it was the last time she would go to a theater. He felt it was a victory of sorts over television. Going back to his car, which he had parked very nearby, he found he had got a ticket, but that didn't dampen his mood.

How beautiful, he thought, "Something is making everything much dimmer." Said so well, the gift was almost worth giving, worth receiving. Her reaction gave the whole thing a final twist. She had turned the tables around. It made for a fitting finish after all. Let them give what they wanted—having said such words she was safe, whole, uncorrupted, on home ground. No matter what happened, no matter how much she watched TV, those words saved her, saved the situation—a little (did he dare say it?) like Galileo's "And yet it moves."

Was he making too much of her remark? Perhaps because he knew her apartment it seemed meaningful to him. The living room had a marble image of Keats on a pedestal, several antique chairs, tables, a chest, books in glass-paneled bookcases, some paintings. It was a room that went the length of the house. One window looked out on the street, the other on a small walled-in garden. There wasn't much light. The patina of time was everywhere. The plain, dark-brown linoleum under the Persian carpets had been there for fifty years: she was so light-footed that it wasn't worn, and, from the many coats of wax, had acquired a polish—an odd effect on such dull material.

The room seemed full of shadows, but if you looked closely, things emerged out of the penumbra, disclosing themselves as in a painting that time and coats of varnish and fumes of candles have made dark. And there she sat, each time he went to see her, pretty, serving the coffee in the finest cups, looking more and more graceful with the years. Her hair was like a little cloud. The imprint of time was on her face, yet she could have been a girl there in the half-light. Her eyes were large and pensive, deep pools reflecting time, and looking larger for the spareness of her face. She was not past blushing. And her hands were active: she wrote many letters, some of these trying to promote plays.

So image a color TV set before her, and watch her, restless, disoriented in her own house, Keats concealed, her books a blur, the paintings blotched out, the silence broken, and the shadow cancelled by this newfangled brightness.

H e r e m e m b e r e d t h e last time he saw her. She had been very ill with a virus and had had a high fever. She was recovering, but looked very frail like a flower that the blade of a sickle has spared. She was sitting on a living room couch. A student nurse was looking after her. "And I didn't die," she said wistfully. "It seems such a waste. I was ready to die but death just passed me by, wouldn't have me, and now I'll have to wait some more, who knows how long. Viral pneumonia—it should have been enough, but it wasn't."

"Oh, don't say that," he told her, and held her by the hand as if to lead her back to life's central path. "The body knows best."

"It doesn't know when to quit." She looked at her cat. "Moonlight has been very good to me, lying close beside me, sometimes on my chest, as if to ease the pain and congestion."

She didn't live alone, but with this cat, Moonlight. He was given her by a friend as a small kitten, six years before, when her former cat—Moonmist—had died. Livio had known Moonmist also, though not from a kitten. Julia had had him for many years before Livio met her, but he didn't think he would ever see, not if he lived as long as she, a more beautiful relationship between a cat and her owner. Owner? The word seemed hardly appropriate. They owned each other. Moonmist was quite irreplaceable, and when he finally died of old age, a little too quickly her friend—the same one who had the idea of buying her the TV—gave her Moonlight. It was a thoughtful initiative, but clumsily timed. It gave the impression that Moonmist could be replaced, the way one replaces an appliance. Also Moonlight wasn't anything like Moonmist in character, though in appearance they were alike, both being Persian and very soft and silvery. The old cat had been wise and restful. The new one jumped all over the place and soon smashed a vase. It was difficult to keep Moonlight confined. But she did her best. And since each year that went by for her was like five for the cat, Moonlight was soon closer to her in age, nearly as close as Moonmist had been. So Livio was glad to hear that Moonlight had sort of nursed Julia in her crisis, and indeed he seemed the image of peace.

Julia, as if knowing this meeting would not recur, asked the student nurse to bring in a little package from another room. She gave it to Livio and he unwrapped it. It contained a very small, old, and rare edition of Petrarch's poems. Here, he thought, was a friend who knew what to give and when to give it. Poetry had knit their friendship, and he vowed it would never unravel.

Her fever was down and the nurse said something about her looking better.

"Have you been watching TV?" Livio asked her.

"Oh dear no!" she said shrugging with horror. "It's there behind the sofa on the floor. I never watch it." She seemed to resent the very presence of it and had it hidden from sight, disposed of, banished. He felt like cheering.

SOON HE LEFT, meaning to return, but never did. He heard about her from Sheila, who sometimes went to visit. Sheila told him that unfortunately Moonlight's good disposition didn't last; he had given Julia's hands, arms and face some deep scratches. Apparently the cat had developed an intense and unaccountable dislike for his mistress, and had finally become so dangerous he had to be taken away.

NOT LONG AFTER that, Julia herself was taken away from her apartment to a nursing home, and her nice old house sold. Still, death kept her waiting for some years.

"She is so listless, just a shadow of her former self," Sheila said to Livio one day. "She is in her nineties, you know. Close to a hundred, I think, and she didn't recognize me. Nor, I must confess, did I recognize her right away, one in a row of very old women in wheelchairs, all with the same expression, or rather lack of expression. She was so distinctive once, so very bright—and now she didn't respond. Only when I mentioned you did her eyes light up, and she repeated your name, Livio, Livio. It was amazing. It was too touching! For a moment, she was herself again. What was it between you two anyway? What went on? She really loves you. You should go to see her. It would be good for her. It would revive her. I don't think anything else will. You must."

ONE DAY, IN the city, he looked for the nursing home, but couldn't find it and soon gave up. Was it that he felt she didn't want to be seen in that place and in that state? He remembered going to Italy to visit his mother just a few months before she died. She was very ill, and a stupid doctor, unable to make a diagnosis, had recommended that her teeth be extracted, on the assumption that they harbored foci of infection. This was done.

There was a delay in readying the dentures for her, and, seeing Livio, she brought both hands in front of her mouth and chin, not to be seen toothless by him.

HE LEARNED OF Julia's death from a telephone message left in his mail box at the college where he taught. It didn't give the name of the person who had left it, just that she remembered him fondly.

LATE IN THE summer, driving home from a party in the town by the sea where the theater had been, on a night that was extraordinarily like that other night, he remembered the kiss, perhaps—no, probably—no, almost certainly—her last passionate kiss, and, for a moment, it all came together, life, under the full moon for whom twenty years are as nothing. Like a lover he left the highway for the back road, and, between the crickets and stars, stopped the car and listened.

Henry David Thoreau

·····························

The Highland Light

THIS LIGHT-HOUSE, known to mariners as the Cape Cod or Highland Light, is one of our "primary sea-coast lights," and is usually the first seen by those approaching the entrance of Massachusetts Bay from Europe. It is forty-three miles from Cape Ann Light, and forty-one from Boston Light. It stands about twenty rods from the edge of the bank, which is here formed of clay. I borrowed the plane and square, level and dividers, of a carpenter who was shingling a barn near by, and using one of those shingles made

---

Henry David Thoreau's legacy was secured with the publication of Walden. Today, many see Thoreau's primary talent as an ecologist. These skills are evident in Cape Cod, his account of visits made to the Cape between 1849 and 1855.

of a mast, contrived a rude sort of quadrant, with pins
for sights and pivots, and got the angle of elevation of
the Bank opposite the light-house, and with a couple
of cod-lines the length of its slope, and so measured
its height on the shingle. It rises one hundred and ten
feet above its immediate base, or about one hundred
and twenty-three feet above mean low water. Graham,
who has carefully surveyed the extremity of the Cape,
makes it one hundred and thirty feet. The mixed sand
and clay lay at an angle of forty degrees with the horizon, where I measured it, but the clay is generally
much steeper. No cow or hen ever gets down it. Half a
mile farther south the bank is fifteen or twenty-five
feet higher, and that appeared to be the highest land in
North Truro. Even this vast clay bank is fast wearing
away. Small streams of water trickling down it at intervals of two or three rods, have left the intermediate
clay in the form of steep Gothic roofs fifty feet high or
more, the ridges as sharp and rugged-looking as rocks;
and in one place the bank is curiously eaten out in the
form of a large semicircular crater.

According to the light-house keeper, the Cape is
wasting here on both sides, though most on the eastern. In some places it had lost many rods within the
last year, and, erelong, the light-house must be moved.
We calculated, from his data, how soon the Cape would
be quite worn away at this point, "for," said he, "I can

remember sixty years back." We were even more surprised at this last announcement,—that is, at the slow waste of life and energy in our informant, for we had taken him to be not more than forty,—than at the rapid wasting of the Cape, and we thought that he stood a fair chance to outlive the former.

Between this October and June of the next year I found that the bank had lost about forty feet in one place, opposite the light-house, and it was cracked more than forty feet farther from the edge at the last date, the shore being strewn with the recent rubbish. But I judged that generally it was not wearing away here at the rate of more than six feet annually. Any conclusions drawn from the observations of a few years or one generation only are likely to prove false, and the Cape may balk expectation by its durability. In some places even a wrecker's foot-path down the bank lasts several years. One old inhabitant told us that when the light-house was built, in 1798, it was calculated that it would stand forty-five years, allowing the bank to waste one length of fence each year, "but," said he, "there it is" (or rather another near the same site, about twenty rods from the edge of the bank).

The sea is not gaining on the Cape everywhere, for one man told me of a vessel wrecked long ago on the north of Provincetown whose "bones" (this was his word) are still visible many rods within the present line of the beach, half buried in sand. Perchance they lie alongside the timbers of a whale. The general statement of the inhabitants is that the Cape is wasting on both sides, but extending itself on particular points on the south and west, as at Chatham and Monomoy Beaches, and at Billingsgate, Long, and Race Points. James Freeman stated in his day that above three miles had been added to Monomoy Beach during the previous fifty years, and it is said to be still extending as fast as ever. A writer in the Massachusetts Magazine, in the last century, tells us that "when the English first settled upon the Cape, there was an island off Chatham, at three leagues' distance, called Webbs' Island, containing twenty acres, covered with red-cedar or savin. The inhabitants of Nantucket used to carry wood from it"; but he adds that in his day a large rock alone marked the spot, and the water was six fathoms deep there. The entrance to Nauset Harbor, which was once in Eastham, has now travelled south into Orleans. The islands in Wellfleet Harbor once formed a continuous beach, though now small vessels pass between them. And so of many other parts of this coast.

Perhaps what the Ocean takes from one part of the Cape it gives to another,—robs Peter to pay Paul. On the eastern side the sea appears to be everywhere encroaching on the land. Not only the land is undermined, and its ruins carried off by currents, but the sand is blown from the beach directly up the steep bank where it is one hundred and fifty feet high, and covers the original surface there many feet deep. If you sit on the edge you will have ocular demonstration of this by soon getting your eyes full. Thus the bank preserves its height as fast as it is worn away. This sand is steadily travelling westward at a rapid rate, "more than a hundred yards," says one writer, within the memory of inhabitants now living; so that in some places peat-meadows are buried deep under the sand, and the peat is cut through it; and in one place a large peat-meadow has made its appearance on the shore in the bank covered many feet deep, and peat has been cut there. This accounts for that great pebble of peat which we saw in the surf. The old oysterman had told us that many years ago he lost a "crittur" by her being mired in a swamp near the Atlantic side east of his house, and twenty years ago he lost the swamp itself entirely, but has since seen signs of it appearing on the beach. He also said that he had seen cedar stumps "as big as cart-wheels" (!) on the bottom of the Bay, three miles off Billingsgate Point, when leaning over the side of his boat in pleasant weather, and that that was dry land not long ago. Another told us that a log canoe known to have been buried many years before on the Bay side at East Harbor in Truro, where the Cape is extremely narrow, appeared at length on the Atlantic side, the Cape having rolled over it, and an old woman said,—"Now, you see, it is true what I told you, that the Cape is moving."

Louise Rafkin

....

Provincetown Diary

YOU HAVE A life. It may even be a big life.

Work: thirty, maybe forty hours every week. Friends: three to ten people whose voices you find on your answering machine weekly or, in times of crisis, daily. A garden: aphids to fight, snails to monitor. You have pets. You have a good dentist. A reliable haircutter. You have a lover. She also has a life.

You write before work, at night, on Saturday mornings. Sending out queries and stories with those fat return

One of many writers nurtured by The Fine Arts Work Center, Louise Rafkin has published numerous works, including Different Daughters: A Book by Mothers of Lesbians (1987), for which she received a 1991 Lambda Literary Award.

envelopes that bug your mailwoman because they won't fit back through the slot without crunching. When people ask you what you do, you name your paying job. Then sometimes, secondly—though you've been published, and though you've been paid, and though you've been doing it for as long as you can remember—you say, "Also, I write."

"Oh, really?"

You say, "Yes." Firmly. But inside it doesn't always feel like you're a writer. It's the paying work that takes the greediest bite of your time. That defines you in so many external ways.

But one day the phone rings and this angel on the other end asks you for a date: seven months on the far side of the country. On a spit of sand you've only read about in *People Magazine* following mention of the Kennedys. Cape Cod. It is morning in your Bay Area apartment; the neighbor's stereo is blasting, and a siren outside has encouraged the local pack of frustrated dogs to begin their daily concert.

"What?"

You won out over several hundred other applicants: You've got a slot at the Fine Arts Work Center in Provincetown. True. You fall to the floor with joy.

Then you call in sick. It's definitely time to use up that sick pay.

Massachusetts. (At first you can't even spell it.)

The Fine Arts Work Center. A winter's worth of free rent, utilities, too. The only place in the country that provides long fellowships to "emerging writers." It's because you're a writer! Ha! You're a *real* writer. Your mother is astounded. She doesn't quite get it—you mean you don't have to *do anything but write?* She calls the relatives nevertheless.

Dump that daily grind of a job. Even a great haircutter can be replaced. (With some difficulty, it turns out.) A lingering good-bye to your lover. (That life she has? She doesn't want to leave it.) Seven free months at the tip of the world can't be passed up.

WE ARRIVE OCTOBER first. It's clear and beautiful in Provincetown. By now the tourists have left and the leaves are beginning to turn. This California girl has never seen such a thing. Just like in the Kodak commercials. Sky divers of yellow and red.

We're shown to our apartments and handed checks ($375 for writers, a tad more for visual artists). As soon as I close the door I burst into sobs. It's not bad, but it's no palace. The second floor of a rickety barn that a realtor would graciously describe as rustic. Paint freckles the walls, green and black mostly, like some version of macabre measles. I can hear each footstep of my upstairs neighbor and the long, sorrowful sigh of the man below. No insulation.

The places are supposed to be furnished, and mine is, in a fashion.

Several hours pass, by which time I've covered the ratty sofa with a favorite piece of fabric, tacked photos of friends and family above my desk, arranged for paint to cover the spattered walls. Dry eyes now. There's a no-pets policy, but I've managed to sneak in my pal Sparky, a California desert tortoise. A beloved state reptile back home, here he's an illegal alien. By the time I'm ready for the first of many unbelievable P-town sunsets, he's resting happily on his electric blanket, snoozing.

THERE ARE TWENTY fellows in residence at the Work Center, ten writers and ten "visuals" as they are soon referred to. Nearly all fellows live on "campus," in a scattering of buildings, studios, and a remodeled lumber-yard near the center of this peculiar town.

Work Center life is vaguely similar to college. There's a communal mail room and nightly get togethers that may include popcorn and ping-pong. This batch of fellows is diverse, ranging in age from early twenties to mid-forties. It's mostly an East Coast lot with several Westerners thrown in. There's a bunch of M.F.A.s; only a few of us hail from the work-a-day world. Several are veterans of the fellowship circuit and know each other from here and there. There are couples and singles and single halves of couples. There are straights and gays and not-so-straights. New couples form and re-form during the long winter months. Thankfully, for the most part, we all get along.

At first the amount of free time is shocking. No work. No commitments to whomever or whatever. But we all slide into some sort of pattern. It seems the "visuals" tend towards late nights, even all-nighters, and the writers are more active during the day. Different parts of the brain perhaps? My downstairs neighbor is a seven a.m. starter. On a manual typewriter. I purchase ear plugs.

I tune into my internal clock. I wake late, nine-ish, breakfast with my boy Spark, and then work until two-ish on fiction. Afternoons I mail submissions and write nonfiction. Some days I don't write at all. I bike, visit new friends. Call on Ruthie at the local thrift store. Read. One week in February turns into a reading marathon. Sometimes I feel guilty about not getting enough done.

Around noon most of us appear in the common room mooning for the mail. Rejections are made more palatable when received in a crowd. They're compared and critiqued. In January, when the stunning autumn is just a picture postcard memory, and the snow and sleet keep us inside longer than we'd care to be, the mail lurkers are downright dangerous. But even those letters full of garbled news about life at my old work place begin to feel like reports from a foreign country. Most everyone in Provincetown is an artist or writer or both. No one you meet here ever asks if you have another job or what you *really* do. But January is hard. It is dark at four o'clock, and one day I'm shocked to find only a single shriveled zucchini at the grocery store. I'm told by the stocker, a poet, "Honey, if you wanted fresh vegetables you should have stayed in California."

Throughout the year we are visited by writers, big names and lesser knowns, some ex-fellows. Sometimes they look at our work or make suggestions. sometimes they come to give a reading, schmooze, get away from city life. We eat potluck dinners and chat. Sometimes this is great. Sometimes it feels like no one really knows what we are supposed to do with one another. The bigwigs aren't here as teachers, but certainly are not peers. Some contacts are made.

Still, much time is spent alone, though there is some exchange between fellows. We swap books, share rides to the nearby library, eat breakfast at the only restaurant that remains open year round. Friendships form across lines of art and literature. For the first time I feel like I'm beginning to understand something about post-modern art. We support each other as we start the spring rotation of readings and gallery shows. I join a biweekly writing group of locals, perfectly suited to my work and needs.

And I fall in love with the town. The way the postmistress knows me and will sometimes plant kisses on those hopeful submissions. The way straight and gay live alongside in nearly equal parts. Some of the straight fellows/fellas find the community a bit daunting (straight single girls discover the pickings slim). Of all the small towns in which to land, I've managed to set down in queer heaven.

People begin to grow anxious after the February thaw. What next? May looms. Fine to be a paid writer, but what gives when the gig is up? Like maniacs, we all submit for residencies, NEAs, teaching positions, whatever. Most apply for a chance at the second year fellowships: Two writers and two artist from all the fellows from all previous years get doled out another slice of pie. The applications are sent off-Cape to an unnamed jury. Some fellows get jobs at the local A&P. The stipends don't seem to quite cover the basics, let alone extras such as car expenses, phone bills, or even health insurance. Most fellows come with some sort of savings.

I've all but decided to return to my old job when the news comes in. I've been gifted another year! There are enviously spoken congratulations. Disappointments. I make plans for a work-a-day summer. On the last Saturday of April the visuals and the writers face off for a highly competitive game of softball. The visuals—who are that day being juried for their second year fellowships—run high on adrenaline and emerge victorious.

The next year passes alongside a new group of fellows. There's a different flavor to this group; they're younger and a bit more ambitious. I'm more integrated with the townsfolk now and sometimes feel like a local. The year passes, much more quickly this time. Some days I have this sense that I have to write everything *now*. That I'll never get this kind of time again. And then other days I just walk in the dunes.

But now it's May and I've finally been given the boot. What really happened? I've completed a collection of stories, published a book of nonfiction and started a novel. More importantly, after fourteen months of being a named writer-in-residence I can see myself as one. Evidence: I declared "writer" on my tax return this year.

It's a shock to be paying rent again. No, I haven't left town. Provincetown is a hard place to leave. When spring comes around there are tulips everywhere. The box turtles come out of hibernation to sun themselves near the ponds at the National Seashore. It's a small seaside town without too many rednecks. Where else can you get all this? Sea, sun, even a super A&P. (Known—of course—as the Gay&P.) There's a flock of us ex-fellows

in town. We work in restaurants and on whale boats and
clean houses and complain about the tourists who pour
down Commercial Street like lemmings. It's a life. A
writer's life.

John Updike

Going Barefoot

WHEN I THINK of the Vineyard, my ankles feel good—bare, airy, lean. Full of bones. I go barefoot there in recollection, and the island as remembered becomes a medley of pedal sensations: the sandy rough planks of Dutcher Dock; the hot sidewalks of Oak Bluffs, followed by the wall-to-wall carpeting of the liquor store; the pokey feel of an accelerator on a naked sole; the hurtful little pebbles of Menemsha Beach and the also hurtful half-buried rocks of Squibnocket; the prickly weeds, virtual cacti, that grew in a certain lawn near Chilmark

---

John Updike *is best known for his novels* Rabbit Run, Marry Me, The Witches of Eastwick *and* Rabbit is Rich, *for which he won the Pulitzer Prize in 1982. This piece is from his 1983 collection,* Hugging the Shore.

Pond; the soft path leading down from this lawn across giving, oozing boards to a bouncy little dock and rowboats that offered another yet friendly texture to the feet; the crystal bit of ocean water; the seethe and suck of a wave tumbling rocks across your toes in its surge back down the sand; sand, the clean wide private sand by Windy Gates and the print-pocked, overused public sand by the boat dock that one kicked around in while waiting for friends to be deferried; the cold steep clay of Gay Head and the flinty littered surface around those souvenir huts that continue to beguile the most jaded child; the startling dew on the grass when one stepped outside with the first cup of coffee to gauge the day's weather; the warmth of the day still lingering in the dunes underfoot as we walked back, Indian-file, through the dark from a beach party and its diminishing bonfire. Going to the post office in bare feet had an infra-legal, anti-totalitarian, comical, gentle feel to it, in the days before the Postal Service moved to the other side of Beetlebung Corner and established itself in a lake of razor-sharp spalls. (When Bill Seward ran the postal annex in his store, it was one of the few spots in the United States that would hand over mail on Sundays.) Shopping at Seward's, one would not so carefreely have shelled out "island prices" for such luxuries as macadamia nuts and candied snails had one been wearing shoes; their absence, like the cashless ease of a charge account, gave a pleasant illusion of unaccountability. The friend of mine who took these photographs used to play golf at Mink Meadows barefoot. My children and I set up a miniature golf course on a turnaround covered with crushed clamshells; after we had been treading this surface for a while, it did not seem too great a transition, even for a middle-aged father of four, to climb a tree barefoot or go walking on a roof. The shingles felt pleasantly peppery, sunbaked.

These are summer memories, mostly August memories; for that's the kind of resident I was. Now it has been some summers since I was even that, and a danger exists of confusing the Vineyard with my children's childhood, which time has swallowed, or with Paradise, from which we have been debarred by well-known angels. Let's not forget the rainy days, the dull days, the cranky-making crowding, and the moldy smell summer furniture gives off when breezes don't blow through the screen door that one keeps meaning to fix, though it's really the landlord's responsibility. Beach pebbles notoriously dry to a disappointing gray on the mantel. The cozy roads and repeated recreations can begin to wear a rut. One wet summer we all, kids and cousins and friends of cousins, kept walking down through poison ivy, not barefoot, to look at a heap of large stones that was either a ninth-century Viking cromlech or a nineteenth-century doghouse, nobody was certain which. Still, there was under it all, fair days and foul, a kicky whiff of freedom, a hint, whispered from the phalanges to the metatarsals, from the calcaneus to the astragalus, that one was free from the mainland's paved oppressions.

Going barefoot is increasingly illegal and does have its dangers. One house we rented overlooked Menemsha Bight from a long porch whose spaced boards had the aligned nicely of harp strings or lines of type in a book. One of my boys, performing some stunt on these boards, rammed splinters into the soles of his feet so deeply a doctor in Edgartown had to cut them out with a surgeon's knife. I wonder if even the most hardened hippies still pad along the tarry streets of Oak Bluffs barefoot as they used to. At Jungle Beach, I remember, nudity spread upward from toes to head and became doctrinaire. But then nudism, interwoven with socialism in the island's history, has always had a doctrinaire side. Being naked approaches being revolutionary; going barefoot is mere populism. "Barefoot boy with cheek of tan" was a rote phrase of my own childhood, quaint even then. But that cliché had once lived and can be seen, not only in illustrations of Mark Twain but also in Winslow Homer's level-eyed etchings and oils of his contemporary America, a place of sandy lanes and soft meadows. There are few places left, even summer places, where one can go barefoot. Too many laws, too much broken glass. On Long Island, the cuffs of one's leisure suit will drag on the ground, and on the Cape, pine needles stick to the feet. Even on Nantucket, those cobblestones are not inviting. But the presiding spirits of Martha's Vineyard, willfully and not without considerable overhead, do preserve this lowly element of our Edenic heritage: treading the earth.

Philip Hamburger

Arriving

ANOTHER SUMMER. BACK to the old house in Wellfleet, on
Cape Cod. Thoreau country. I think of "Little Gidding," from
Eliot's "Four Quartets":

> And the end of all our exploring
> Will be to arrive where we started
> And know the place for the first time.

I open the door, glance around the old rooms, experience the strange sensation that I have been away not an entire
winter but about twenty minutes. Old familiar steep and narrow

---

*Short story writer Philip Hamburger's "Arriving" first appeared in The
New Yorker in July of 1995.*

staircase, old familiar pictures: the print of Ibsen; the print
of the overfed, much too contented cat; the cherished oils
of beach and woods by friends and neighbors.

Hey, buddy, knock off the aesthetics! Get real.
You've got problems. Raccoons have been in the attic, living
it up like Donald Trump. Smartest little creatures east of
the Mississippi. Could run the whole damn country, just
with their prehensile thumbs. I call the raccoon man for
help; says he'll come. There's a dead mouse somewhere
under the house, making its presence known. A domesti-
cated squirrel, nowhere to be seen, has been dining on a
window frame in the sitting room, near the Audubon
reproduction of the belted kingfishers. (The female is swal-
lowing a fish.) The squirrel has almost shaved down the
muntins. My wife has gone upstairs. "Toilet's on the fritz!"
she calls down. "Get the plumber!" (The equivalent of
finding Jimmy Hoffa.) Mirabile dictu, I reach the plumber.
"Look, Skipper,"he says. "That toilet went through the
Great Depression. That toilet is a dead toilet—once gulped
five gallons of water every flush. I'll give you something
new—flushes only a gallon and a half and you'll win an
environmental medal." I order the toilet. Then I discover
we're out of propane gas, but the gas man can't get his
truck here until we clear away a giant felled beech tree that
blocks the road to the tank. And there's bright-yellow pine
pollen deeply settled everywhere. It's gesundheit time at
the old homestead, and I forage for Kleenex.

To hell with dead mice, hungry squirrels, high-I.Q. raccoons, and pollen, too. Feel sudden need to reconnect with the outdoors. Take twenty-minute walk down to the Atlantic Ocean. Pass gleaming freshwater kettle-hole ponds, left over from glacial times. Pass small Herring River, and spy darting schools of alewives that have been spawning in nearby Gull Pond and are now heading toward Massachusetts Bay and the open ocean, so that, as the legend goes, they can make their annual trip back to Norway and joyous smorgasbords. Beach grass waving silkily, wild roses clumped near beach, beach itself, and high dunes, in resilient form. Walk back from the beach and reach the Old King's Highway. Some say that it ran from Boston to Provincetown, and if you look closely you can see deep ruts left by carts and carriages in bygone times.

Back to the house. A thousand bees are swarming around, near an attic window. They have been away two, three years, but apparently the queen also missed the old place and decided to come home. In a sense, I'm in Heaven. Perhaps I'm a bee. I think of Emily Dickinson:

> The Pedigree of Honey
> Does not concern the Bee—
> A Clover, any time, to him,
> Is Aristocracy.

Benjamin Franklin

....

The Provincetown Sea Monster

BOSTON, SEPTEMBER 28, 1719. On the 17 Instant there appear'd in Cape-Cod harbour a strange creature, His head like a Lyons, with very large Teeth, Ears hanging down, a large Beard, a long Beard, with curling hair on his head, his Body about 16 foot long, a round buttock, with a short Tayle of a yellowish colour, the Whale boats gave him chase, he was very fierce and gnashed his teeth with great rage when they attackt him, he was shot at 3 times and Wounded, when he rose out of the Water he always faced the boats in that angry manner, the

---

The uncle of the famous patriot and inventor, this Ben Franklin is believed to be responsible for much journalistic sensationalism, including his The Provincetown Sea Monster.

Harpaniers struck at him, but in vaine, for after 5 hours chase, he took him to see again. None of the people ever saw his like befor.

Timothy Alden

....

Maushop's Smoke

IN FORMER TIMES, a great many moons ago, a bird, extraordinary for its size, used often to visit the south shore of Cape Cod, and carry from thence to the southward, a vast number of small children.

Maushop, who was an Indian giant, as fame reports, resided in these parts. Enraged at the havock among the children, he, on a certain time, waded into the sea in pursuit of the bird, till he had crossed the sound and reached Nantucket. Before Maushop forded the sound, the island was unknown to the aborigines of America.

Much Native American history has been stripped from the Cape; it remains mostly in place names and souvenirs. Timothy Alden tells the classic 18th-century Wampanoag tale of Maushop, the man turned into a great white whale.

Tradition says, that Maushop found the bones of the children in a heap under a large tree. He then wishing to smoke a pipe, ransacked the island for tobacco; but finding none, filled his pipe with poke, a weed which the Indians sometimes used as its substitute. Ever since the above memorable event, fogs have been frequent at Nantucket and on the Cape. In allusion to this tradition, when the aborigines observed a fog rising, they would say, "There comes old Maushop's smoke."

Sylvia Plath

Mussel Hunter at Rock Harbor

I CAME BEFORE the water—
Colorists came to get the
Good of the Cape light that scours
Sand grit to sided crystal
And buffs and sleeks the blunt hulls
Of the three fishing smacks beached
On the bank of the river's

Backtracking tail. I'd come for

Sylvia Plath was born and raised in New England before moving to England in
the late 1950s. Her first volume of poetry, The Colossus, appeared in 1960;
her famous novel, The Bell Jar, was published in 1963. She died, by suicide,
the same year.

Free fish-bait: the blue mussels
Clumped like bulbs at the grass-root
Margin of the tidal pools.
Dawn tide stood dead low. I smelt
Mud stench, shell guts, gulls' leavings;
Heard a queer crusty scrabble

Cease, and I neared the silenced
Edge of a cratered pool-bed
The mussels hung dull blue and
Conspicuous, yet it seemed
A sly world's hinges had swung
Shut against me. All held still.
Though I counted scant seconds,

Enough ages lapsed to win
Confidence of safe-conduct
In the wary otherworld
Eyeing me. Grass put forth claws;
Small mud knobs, nudged from under,
Displaced their domes as tiny
Knights might doff their casques. The crabs

Inched from their pigmy burrows
And from the trench-dug mud, all
Camouflaged in mottled mail
Of browns and greens. Each wore one

Claw swollen to a shield large
As itself—no fiddler's arm
Grown Gargantuan by trade,

But grown grimly, and grimly
Borne, for a use beyond my
Guessing of it. Sibilant
Mass-motived hordes, they sidled
Out in a converging stream
Toward the pool-mouth, perhaps to
Meet the thin and sluggish thread

Of sea retracing its tide-
Way up the river-basin.
Or to avoid me. They moved
Obliquely with a dry-wet
Sound, with a glittery wisp
And trickle. Could they feel mud
Pleasurable under claws

As I could between bare toes?
That question ended it—I
Stood shut out, for once, for all,
Puzzling the passage of their
Absolutely alien
Order as I might puzzle
At the clear tail of Halley's

Comet coolly giving my
Orbit the go-by, made known
By a family name it
Knew nothing of. So the crabs
Went about their business, which
Wasn't fiddling, and I filled
A big handkerchief with blue

Mussels. From what the crabs saw,
If they could see, I was one
Two-legged mussel-picker.
High on the airy thatching
Of the dense grasses I found
The husk of a fiddler-crab,
Intact, strangely strayed above

His world of mud—green color
And innards bleached and blown off
Somewhere by much sun and wind;
There was no telling if he'd
Died recluse or suicide
Or headstrong Columbus crab.
The crab-face, etched and set there,

Grimaced as skulls grimace: it
Had an Oriental look,
A samurai death mask done

On a tiger tooth, less for
Art's sake than God's. Far from sea—
Where red-freckled crab-backs, claws
And whole crabs, dead, their soggy

Bellies pallid and upturned,
Perform their shambling waltzes
On the waves' dissolving turn
And return, losing themselves
Bit by bit to their friendly
Element—this relic saved
Face, to face the bald-faced sun.

Alice May Brock

Ciro & Sal's Recipes

THERE ARE CERTAIN moments, certain places, that stick
in your mind, that become guidelines, the ultimate experience that all others are compared with, and, of course, fall
short of.

I spent my first twelve summers in Provincetown on
Cape Cod. My father worked with a fellow up there named
Peter Hunt who owned a whole alleyway of shops. One
summer, a little coffee and sandwich place—an outdoor
café—appeared in the alley. My only interest in it was that
my "boyfriend's" mother worked there. It was owned by

*Arguably the most famous dining spot on the Cape, Ciro & Sal's Provincetown
restaurant combines home-grown artistry with culinary excellence. Alice May
Brock divulges the secrets of their Cape cuisine.*

two artists, Ciro Cozzi and Sal Del Deo. Shortly after they opened up, I stopped going to Provincetown. I was a teenager and wanted to stay in Brooklyn with the guys and go to Coney Island.

I went back to Provincetown when I was about eighteen. My father gave me fifty dollars to rent a bike, buy flipper dough and eat at Ciro and Sal's on Wednesday night. The special was "Cacciucco Livornese"—whole lobster, chicken, cherrystone clams, mussels and other varieties of seafood, baked in a light sauce of tomato, wine and herbs, en casserole. Being a dutiful daughter and mostly because my father knew what was good, I went—down the old Peter Hunt Alley, into a courtyard, down a few stone steps, into a tiny room sparkling with candles, and filled with the most wonderful smells my nose had ever encountered. I sat down at a tiny table on a very uncomfortable nail keg and ordered the special. What happened after that is history. I've never forgotten that meal. It was one of the first I had had the pleasure of eating alone and uninterrupted. I closed my eyes, I rocked in ecstasy; I sucked on mussel shells and rolled rice and sauce around in my mouth. It was heaven. I remember discussing the food with my sister, who had done the same thing. We were in awe.

Then a few more years passed. I opened and closed my first restaurant. And one April evening I found myself back in Provincetown. I went to Ciro's. It was bigger, and they had a liquor license, but the smells were the same—wonderful. I went upstairs and sat alone in a corner. I ordered a bottle of wine, a pile of steamed mussels and an order of fried zucchini. Life once again took on new dimensions. I asked the waiter—Dennis was his name—how the veal was. "We are famous for our veal." Great! I ordered another bottle of wine, and "Veal Piccata—scallops of veal with mushrooms, lemon and cream." Dennis thought it was too much. "Don't worry, sweetheart, I can handle it."

After dinner I was in seventh heaven, a bit crocked, and I sent a note down to the kitchen. I don't remember now the exact wording, but it was a love note. I wrote that I had eaten there when I was younger, and I had never forgotten it. Since then I had opened a restaurant myself and was inspired by Ciro and Sal's. I signed it "Alice of Alice's Restaurant," something I had never done before.

Dennis came back up with my brandy, followed by Ciro and everybody else who worked there. There was lots of brandy and laughing and hugging and smiling and kissing as Ciro and I talked about veal with such zeal that we finally lunged at each other across the table, screaming ravioli, cannelloni and spinach noodles, and zuppa di pesce. All in all, it was a wonderful meeting.

Cacciucco Alla Livornese

Fish Stew with Capers and Fresh Herbs

Serves 4

1 1 1/2-pound chicken, cut into 10 or 12 pieces

1/2 cup olive oil

3 garlic cloves, peeled

1/4 cup red wine vinegar

1/4 cup dry white wine

Salt and freshly ground black pepper

3 cups Marinara sauce

1 tablespoon capers, rinsed and drained

1 tablespoon chopped fresh basil leaves

1 teaspoon chopped fresh rosemary leaves

2 tablespoons finely chopped fresh parsley leaves

1 1 3/4-pound lobster

8 littleneck clams, washed

12 mussels, washed and debearded

1 pound haddock or cod

8 shrimp, shelled and deveined

2 squid, cleaned and sliced into 1/4-inch rings

Preheat the oven to 400 degrees.

Heat the oil in a skillet. Add the chicken and the garlic and brown the chicken on both sides. Lower the heat and add the vinegar, wine, salt and pepper. Cook until the chicken is almost done then remove and set aside. Discard the garlic.

Add the Marinara sauce, capers, basil, rosemary and 1 tablespoon of the parsley to the skillet. Simmer for 5 minutes.

Transfer the sauce to a roasting pan and add the lobster, clams and mussels to the pan. Place the pan over two burners on top of the stove. Cover the pan and cook for 15 minutes.

Place the fish, shrimp and squid in another skillet. Add 1 cup of the sauce from the lobster pan. Cover the skillet and cook over medium heat, being careful not to overcook. The fish and shellfish should be slightly underdone.

Combine the chicken, fish, shrimp and squid in the roasting pan with the lobster, clams and mussels. Cover the pan with aluminum foil and bake for 10 minutes.

Remove the pan from the oven. Crack the lobster claws and split the tail. Arrange the remaining seafood and chicken on a large serving dish. Arrange the lobster pieces on top and pour about 2 cups of the sauce over all. Sprinkle the remaining tablespoon of parsley on top.

Shebnah Rich

....

Provincetown

FORTY YEARS AGO the shores of Provincetown were lined with wind-mills, called in the vernacular, "salt-mills," used for pumping ocean water into the hundreds of acres of "salt works" that completely flanked the town and came up almost into their houses and bed-chambers. What with the salt ocean rolling on the back side, the salt bay washing the front, the thousands of hogsheads of pure salt crystallizing in shallow vats or high piled in storehouses, waiting market, and miles of salt codfish curing the autumnal sun, Provincetown could lay good claim to being a well-preserved community. A view

---

Shebnah Rich was born in Truro in 1824, but only summered on the Cape, living most of his life in Boston. He wrote Truro—Cape Cod in 1883, following a long career as a merchant.

of the town is better worth seeing from any approach than hundreds of places of wider fame, but fifty years ago an approach at highwater from Truro, the only land communication, was a rare view.

The quaint village hugging the crescent shore for three miles, hundreds of mills from the shore, wharves and hill-tops all in lively motion and commotion, the tall spars of the vessels in port, the steep hills rising like huge earth-works of defence, and the low sandy point half-coiled around the harbor, anchored at the tip by the lighthouse of old Darby fame, was a sight that could be seen nowhere else in this land, and was more like the old Dutch and Flemish pictures of Hobbema and Van Ostade than anything I have seen. About this time a profane visitor wrote in a weekly newspaper, "Houses, salt-works, and curiously-built hovels, for uses unknown, are mixed up together. It would seem that the God of the infidels, which they call chance, had a hand in this mysterious jumble." The citizens properly resented this fling at the practical architecture, and intimated they knew their own business.

In 1829, the Provincetown minister, Mr. Stone, said to Dr. Cornell, then a Wellfleet schoolmaster, "Would you believe that there is a town in the United States with 1800 inhabitants and only one horse with one eye? Well, that town is Provincetown and I am the only man in town that owns a horse and he is an old white one with one eye." . . .

There was then no road through the town. With
no cars, wagons, carriages, horses or oxen, why a road?
A road was well enough where there was use for it. The
first sleigh ever used in the town was a dory; a good
substitute and suggestion for the North Pole explorers. A
Provincetown boy seeing a carriage driving through the
town wondered how she could steer so straight without
a rudder. . . . Here every man had a path from his house
to his boat or vessel, and once launched, he was on the
broad highway of nations, without tax or toll. There
were paths to the neighbors, paths to school, and paths
to church; tortuous, perhaps, but they were good pilots
by night or day, on land or water. Besides, at lowwater
there was a road such as none else could boast, washed
completely twice a day from year to year, wide enough
and free enough and long enough, if followed, for the
armies of the Netherlands.

> For you, they said, no barriers be,
> For you no sluggard rest;
> Each street leads downward to the sea
> Or landward to the West.

The cob wharves were then not as frequent or
long as now, and travel passed under and around them.
Washing fish is one of the cherished institutions of
Provincetown. It might not inappropriately be adopted as

her coat of arms. The division of the United States surplus revenue was the beginning of a new era in Provincetown. When the question of appropriating the money for laying out a road and building a sidewalk through the town was being discussed, a citizen in town meeting said: "As this money has proved a bone of contention in most places, I think the best place for bones is under our feet; I am therefore in favor of appropriating this fund to a sidewalk throughout the town." Like all great improvements, it met with bitter opposition. The old were wed to old ways and content. They had known no inconveniences. Houses, stores, saltworks, fish flakes and mills were to be removed, wells to be filled, and rough places made smooth, before the road could be laid out and sidewalks built. All of which was done, and the five-plank walk on one side of the street, the whole length of the town, substantially as now, was opened for travel in February, 1838, at a cost of two thousand dollars. Tradition says that some of the old people, particularly the ladies, who had strenuously opposed the project, declared they would never walk on it, and were as good as their word, walking slip-shod through the sand as long as they lived. In some of the old pictures the people are represented without feet, it being understood so much was covered by the sand.

Kurt Vonnegut

....

The Hyannis Port Story

THE FARTHEST WAY from home I ever sold a storm window was in Hyannis Port, Massachusetts, practically in the front yard of President Kennedy's summer home. My field of operation is usually within about twenty-five miles of my home, which is in North Crawford, New Hampshire.

The Hyannis Port thing happened because somebody misunderstood something I said, and thought I was an ardent Goldwater Republican. Actually, I hadn't made up my mind one way or the other about Goldwater.

Long-time Cape resident Kurt Vonnegut has written numerous novels and short stories, but is perhaps best remembered for Slaughterhouse Five (1969). "The Hyannis Port Story" displays Vonnegut's penchant for social satire and science fiction.

What happened was this: The program chairman of the North Crawford Lions Club was a Goldwater man, and he had this college boy named Robert Taft Rumfoord come talk to a meeting one day about the Democratic mess in Washington and Hyannis Port. The boy was national president of some kind of student organization that was trying to get the country back to what he called First Principles. One of the First Principles, I remember, was getting rid of the income tax. You should have heard the applause.

I got a funny feeling that the boy didn't care much more about politics than I did. He had circles under his eyes, and he looked as though he'd just as soon be somewhere else. He would say strong things, but they came out sounding like music on a kazoo. The only time he got really interesting was when he told about being in sailboat races and golf and tennis matches with different Kennedys and their friends. He said that there was a lot of propaganda around about what a fine golfer Bobby Kennedy was, whereas Bobby actually couldn't golf for sour apples. He said Pierre Salinger was one of the worst golfers in the world, and didn't care for sailing or tennis at all.

Robert Taft Rumfoord's parents were there to hear him. They had come all the way from Hyannis Port. They were both very proud of him—or at least the father was. The father had on white flannel trousers and white shoes, even though there was snow on the ground, and a double-breasted blue coat with brass buttons. The boy introduced him as *Commodore* William Rumfoord. The Commodore was a short man with very shaggy eyebrows and pale blue eyes. He looked like a gruff, friendly teddybear, and so did his son. I found out later, from a Secret Service man, that the Kennedys sometimes called the Rumfoords *"the Pooh people,"* on account of they were so much like the bear in the children's book *Winnie the Pooh.*

The Commodore's wife wasn't a Pooh person, though. She was thin and quick, and maybe two inches taller than the Commodore. Bears have a way of looking as though they're pretty much satisfied with everything. The Commodore's lady didn't have that look. I could tell she was jumpy about a lot of things.

After the boy was through pouring fire and brimstone on the Kennedys, with his father applauding everything he said, Hay Boyden, the building mover stood up. He was a Kennedy Democrat, and he said some terrible things to the boy. The only one I remember is the first thing he said: "Son, if you keep blowing off steam like this during your Boy Scout days, you aren't going to have an ounce of pressure left when you're old enough to vote." It got worse from there on.

The boy didn't get mad. He just got embarrassed, and answered back with some more kazoo music. It was the Commodore who really cared. He turned the color of tomato juice. He stood up and he argued back, did it pretty well, even though his wife was pulling at the bottom of his brass-buttoned coat the whole time. She was trying to get him to stop raising such an uproar, but the Commodore loved the uproar.

The meeting broke up with practically everybody embarrassed, and I went over to Hay Boyden to talk to him about something that didn't have anything to do with Kennedy or Goldwater. It was about a bathtub enclosure I had sold him. He had insisted on installing it himself, saving himself about seven dollars and a half. Only it leaked, and his dining-room ceiling fell down, and Hay claimed that was the fault of the merchandise and not the installation. Hay had some poison left in his system from his argument with the boy, so he used it up on me. I answered him back with the truth, and walked away from him, and Commodore Rumfoord grabbed my hand and shook it. He thought I'd been defending his boy and Barry Goldwater.

"What business you in?" he asked me.

I told him, and, the next thing I knew, I had an order for storm windows all around on a four-story house in Hyannis Port.

The Commodore called that big old house a cottage.

*

"You're a Commodore in the Navy?" I asked him.

"No," he said. "My father, however, was Secretary of the Navy under William Howard Taft. That's my full name: Commodore William Howard Taft Rumfoord."

"You're in the Coast Guard?" I said.

"You mean the *Kennedy Private Fleet?*" he said.

"Pardon me?" I said.

"That's what they ought to call the Coast Guard these days," he said, "Its sole mission seems to be to protect Kennedys while they water-ski behind high-powered stinkpots."

"You're *not* in the Coast Guard?" I said. I couldn't imagine what was left.

"I was commodore of the Hyannis Port Yacht Club in 1946," he said.

He didn't smile, and neither did I, and neither did his wife, whose name was Clarice. But Clarice *did* give a little sigh that sounded like the whistle on a freight train far, far away on a wet morning.

I didn't know what the trouble was at the time, but Clarice was sighing because the Commodore hadn't held any job of any description since 1946. Since then, he'd made a full-time career of raging about whoever was President of the United States, including Eisenhower.

Especially Eisenhower.

So I went down to Hyannis Port in my truck to measure the Commodore's windows late in June. His driveway was on Irving Avenue. So was the Kennedys' driveway. And President Kennedy and I hit Cape Cod on the very same day.

Traffic to Hyannis Port was backed up through three villages. There were license plates from every state in the Republic. The line was moving about four miles an hour. I was passed by several groups of fifty-mile hikers. My radiator came to a boil four times.

I was feeling pretty sorry for myself, because I was just an ordinary citizen, and had to get stuck in lines like that. But then I recognized the man in the limousine up ahead of me. It was Adlai Stevenson. He wasn't moving any faster than I was, and his radiator was boiling, too.

One place there, we got stuck so long that Mr. Stevenson and I got out and walked around a little. I took the opportunity to ask him how the United Nations were getting along. He told me they were getting along about as well as could be expected. That wasn't anything I didn't already know.

When I finally got to Hyannis Port, I found out Irving Avenue was blocked off by police and Secret Service men. Adlai Stevenson got to go down it, but I didn't. The police made me get back into line with the tourists, who were being shunted down a street one block over from Irving Avenue.

The next thing I knew, I was in Hyannis, going past the *Presidential Motor Inn*, the *First Family Waffle Shop*, the *PT-109 Cocktail Lounge*, and a miniature golf course called the *New Frontier*.

I went into the waffle shop, and I called up the Rumfoords to find out how an ordinary storm-window salesman was supposed to get down Irving Avenue without dying in a hail of lead. It was the butler I talked to. He took down my license number, and found out how tall I was and what color my eyes were and all. He said he would tell the Secret Service, and they would let me by next time.

It was late in the afternoon, and I'd missed lunch, so I decided to have a waffle. All the different kinds of waffles were named after Kennedys and their friends and relatives. A waffle with strawberries and cream was a *Jackie*. A waffle with a scoop of ice cream was a *Caroline*. They even had a waffle named *Arthur Schlesinger, Jr.*

I had a thing called a *Teddy*—and a cup of *Joe*.

I GOT THROUGH next time, went right down Irving Avenue behind the Defense Minister of Pakistan. Except for us, that street was as quiet as a stretch of the Sahara Desert.

There wasn't anything to see at all on the President's side, except for a new, peeled-cedar fence about eight feet high and two hundred feet long, with a gate in it. The Rumfoord cottage faced the gate from across the street. It was the biggest house, and one of the oldest, in the village. It was stucco. It had towers and balconies, and a veranda that ran around all four sides.

On a second-floor balcony was a huge portrait of Barry Goldwater. It had bicycle reflectors in the pupils of its eyes. Those eyes stared right through the Kennedy gate. There were floodlights all around it, so I could tell it was lit up at night. And the floodlights were rigged with blinkers.

A MAN WHO sells storm windows can never be really sure about what class he belongs to, especially if he installs the windows, too. So I was prepared to keep out from under foot, and go about my business, measuring the windows. But the Commodore welcomed me like a guest of great importance. He invited me to cocktails and dinner, and to spend the night. He said I could start measuring the next day.

So we had martinis out on the veranda. Only we didn't sit on the most pleasant side, which looked out on the Yacht Club dock and the harbor. We sat on the side that looked out on all the poor tourists being shunted off toward Hyannis. The Commodore liked to talk about all those fools out there.

"Look at them!" he said. "They wanted glamour, and now they realize they're not going to get it. They actually expected to be invited to play touch football with Eunice and Frank Sinatra and the Secretary of Health and Welfare. Glamour is what they voted for, and look at 'em now. They don't even get to look at a Kennedy chimney up above the trees. All the glamour they'll get out of this administration is an overpriced waffle named *Caroline*."

A helicopter went over, very low, and it landed somewhere inside the Kennedy fence. Clarice said she wondered who it was.

"Pope John the Sixth," said the Commodore.

The butler, whose name was John, came out with a big bowl. I thought it was peanuts or popcorn, but it turned out to be Goldwater buttons. The Commodore had John take the bowl out to the street, and offer buttons to the people in cars. A lot of people took them. Those people were disappointed. They were sore.

Some fifty-mile hikers, who'd actually hiked sixty-seven miles, all the way from Boston, asked if they could please lie down on the Rumfoord lawn for a while. They were burned up, too. They thought it was the duty of the President, or at least the Attorney General, to thank them for walking so far. The Commodore said they could not only lie down, but he would give them lemonade, if they would put on Goldwater buttons. They were glad to.

"Commodore," I said, "where's that nice boy of yours, the one who talked to us up in New Hampshire."

"The one who talked to you is the only one I got," he said.

"He certainly poured it on," I said.

"Chip off the old block," he said.

Clarice gave that faraway freight-whistle sigh of hers again.

"The boy went swimming just before you got here," said the Commodore. "He should be back at any time, unless he's been decapitated by a member of the Irish Mafia on water skis."

We went around to the water side of the veranda to see if we could catch sight of young Robert Taft Rumfoord in swimming. There was a Coast Guard cutter out there, shooing tourists in motorboats away from the Kennedy beach. There was a sightseeing boat crammed with people gawking in our direction. The barker on the boat had a very loud loudspeaker, and we could hear practically everything he said.

"*The white boat there is the Honey Fitz, the President's personal yacht,*" said the barker. "*Next to it is the Marlin, which belongs to the President's father, Joseph C. Kennedy, former Ambassador to the Court of St. James.*"

"The President's stinkpot, and the President's father's stinkpot," said the Commodore. He called all motorboats stinkpots. "This is a harbor that should be devoted exclusively to sail."

There was a chart of the harbor on the veranda

wall. I studied it, and found a Rumfoord Point, a Rumfoord Rock, and a Rumfoord Shoal. The Commodore told me his family had been in Hyannis Port since 1884.

"There doesn't seem to be anything named after the Kennedys," I said.

"Why *should* there be?" he said. "They only got here day before yesterday."

"Day before yesterday?" I said.

And he asked me, "What would *you* call nineteen-twenty-one?"

"No, sir," the barker said to one of his passengers, "*that is not the President's house. Everybody asks that. That great big ugly stucco house, folks, that's the Rumfoord Cottage. I agree with you, it's too big to be called* cottage, *but you know how rich people are.*"

"Demoralized and bankrupt by confiscatory taxation," said the Commodore. "You know," he said, "it isn't as though Kennedy was the first President we ever had in Hyannis Port. Taft, Harding, Coolidge, and Hoover were all guests of my father in this very house. Kennedy is simply the first President who's seen fit to turn the place into an eastern enclave of *Disneyland.*"

"No, mam," said the barker, "*I don't know where the Rumfoords get their money, but they don't have to work at all, I know that. They just sit on that porch there, and drink martinis, and let the old mazooma roll in.*"

The Commodore blew up. He said he was going to sue the owners of the sight-seeing boat for a blue million. His wife tried to calm him down, but he made me come into his study with him while he called up his lawyers.

"You're a witness," he said.

BUT HIS TELEPHONE rang before he could call his lawyers. The person who was calling him was a Secret Service Agent named Raymond Boyle. I found out later that Boyle was known around the Kennedy household as the Rumfoord *Specialist* or the *Ambassador to Rumfoordiana.* Whenever anything came up that had to do with the Rumfoords, Boyle had to handle it.

The Commodore told me to go upstairs and listen in on the extension in the hall. "This will give you an idea of how arrogant civil servants have become these days," he said.

So I went upstairs.

"The Secret Service is one of the least secret services I've ever come in contact with," the Commodore was saying when I picked up the phone. "I've seen drum and bugle corps that were less obtrusive. Did I ever tell you about the time Calvin Coolidge, who was also a President, as it happened, went fishing for scup with my father and me off the end of the Yacht Club dock?"

"Yessir, you have, many times," said Boyle. "It's a good story, and I want to hear it again sometime. But right now I'm calling about your son."

The Commodore went right ahead with the story anyway. "President Coolidge," he said, "insisted on baiting his own hook, and the combined Atlantic and Pacific Fleets were not anchored offshore, and the sky was not black with airplanes, and brigades of Secret Service Agents were not trampling the neighbors' flowerbeds to purée."

"Sir—" said Boyle patiently, "your son Robert was apprehended in the act of boarding the President's father's boat, the *Marlin*."

"Back in the days of Coolidge, there *were* no stinkpots like that in this village, dribbling petroleum products, belching fumes, killing the fish, turning the beaches a gummy black."

"Commodore Rumfoord, sir," said Boyle, "did you hear what I said about your son?"

"Of course," said the Commodore. "You said Robert, a member of the Hyannis Port Yacht Club, was caught touching a vessel belonging to another member of the club. This may seem a very terrible crime to a landlubber like yourself; but it has long been a custom of the sea, Mr. Boyle, that a swimmer, momentarily fatigued, may, upon coming to a vessel not his own, grasp that vessel and rest, without fear of being fired upon by the Coast Guard, or of having his fingers smashed by members of the Secret Service, or, as I prefer to call them, the *Kennedy Palace Dragoons*."

"There has been no shooting, and no smashing, sir," said Boyle "There has also been no evidence of swimmer's fatigue. Your Robert went up the anchor line of the *Marlin* like a chimpanzee. He *swarmed* up that rope, Commodore. I believe that's the proper nautical term. And I remind you, as I tried to remind him, that persons moving, uninvited, unannounced, with such speed and purposefulness within the vicinity of a President are, as a matter of time-honored policy, to be turned back at all costs—to be turned back, if need be, *violently*."

"Was it a Kennedy who gave the order that the boarder be repelled?" the Commodore wanted to know.

"There was no Kennedy on board, sir."

"The stinkpot was unoccupied?"

"Adlai Stevenson and Walter Reuther and one of my men were on board, sir," said Boyle. "They were all below, until they heard Robert's feet hit the deck."

"Stevenson and Reuther?" said the Commodore. "That's the last time I let my son go swimming without a dagger in his teeth. I hope he was opening the sea-cocks when beaten insensible by truncheons."

"Very funny, sir," said Boyle, his voice developing a slight cutting edge.

"You're sure it was my Robert?" said the Commodore.

"Who else but your Robert wears a Goldwater button on his swimming trunks?" asked Boyle.

"You object to his political views?" the Commodore demanded.

"I mention the button as a means of identification. Your son's politics do not interest the Secret Service. For your information, I spent seven years protecting the life of a Republican, and three protecting the life of a Democrat," said Boyle.

"For your information, Mr. Boyle," said the Commodore, "Dwight David Eisenhower was not a Republican."

"Whatever he was, I protected him," said Boyle. "He may have been a Zoroastrian, for all I know. And whatever the next President is going to be, I'll protect him, too. I also protect the lives of persons like your son from the consequences of excessive informality where the Presidential presence is concerned." Now Boyle's voice really started to cut. It sounded like a bandsaw working on galvanized tin. "I tell you, officially and absolutely unsmilingly now, your son is to cease and desist from using Kennedy boats as love nests."

That got through to the Commodore, bothered him. "Love nests?" he said.

"Your Robert has been meeting a girl on boats all over the harbor," said Boyle. "He arranged to meet her today on the *Marlin*. He was sure it would be vacant. Adlai Stevenson and Walter Reuther were a shock."

The Commodore was quiet for a few seconds, and then he said, "Mr. Boyle, I resent your implications. If I ever hear of your implying such a thing about my son to anyone else, you had better put your pistol and shoulder holster in your wife's name, because I'll sue you for everything you've got. My Robert has never gone with a girl he wasn't proud to introduce to his mother and me, and he never will."

"You're going to meet this one any minute now," said Boyle. "Robert is on his way home with her."

The Commodore wasn't tough at all now. He was uneasy and humble when he said, "Would you mind telling me her name?"

"Kennedy, sir," said Boyle, "Sheila Kennedy, fresh over from Ireland, a fourth cousin of the President of the United States."

Robert Taft Rumfoord came in with the girl right after that, and announced they were engaged to be married.

SUPPER THAT NIGHT in the Rumfoord cottage was sad and beautiful and happy and strange. There were Robert and his girl, and me, and the Commodore and his lady.

That girl was so intelligent, so warm, and so beautiful that she broke my heart every time I looked at her. That was why supper was so peculiar. The girl was so desirable, and the love between her and Robert was so sweet and clean, that nobody could think of anything but silly little things to say. We mainly ate in silence.

The Commodore brought up the subject of politics just once. He said to Robert, "Well—uh—will you still be making speeches around the country, or—uh—"

"I think I'll get out of politics entirely for a while," said Robert.

The Commodore said something that none of us could understand, because the words sort of choked him.

"Sir?" said Robert.

"I said," said the Commodore, " 'I would think you would.' "

I looked at the Commodore's lady, at Clarice. All the lines had gone out of her face. She looked young and beautiful too. She was completely relaxed for the first time in God-knows-how-many years.

ONE OF THE things I said that supper was was sad. The sad part was how empty and quiet it left the Commodore.

The two lovers went for a moonlight sail. The Commodore and his lady and I had brandy on the veranda, on the water side. The sun was down. The tourist traffic had petered out. The fifty-mile hikers who had asked to rest on the lawn that afternoon were still all there, sound asleep, except for one boy who played a guitar. He played it slowly. Sometimes it seemed like a minute between the time he would pluck a string and the time he would pluck one again.

John, the butler, came out and asked the Commodore if it was time to turn on Senator Goldwater's floodlights yet.

"I think we'll just leave him off tonight, John," said the Commodore.

"Yes, sir," said John.

"I'm still for him, John," said the Commodore. "Don't anybody misunderstand me. I just think we ought to give him a rest tonight."

"Yes, sir," said John, and he left.

It was dark on the veranda, so I couldn't see the Commodore's face very well. The darkness, and the brandy, and the slow guitar let him start telling the truth about himself without feeling much pain.

"Let's give the Senator from Arizona a rest," he said. "Everybody knows who he is. The question is: Who am I?"

"A lovable man," said Clarice in the dark.

"With Goldwater's floodlights turned off, and with my son engaged to marry a Kennedy, what am I but what the man on the sight-seeing boat said I was: A man who sits on this porch, drinking martinis, and letting the old mazooma roll in."

"You're an intelligent, charming, well-educated man, and you're still quite young," said Clarice.

"I've got to find some kind of work." he said.

"We'll both be so much happier," she said. "I would love you, no matter what. But I can tell you now, darling—its awfully hard for a woman to admire a man who actually doesn't do anything."

We were dazzled by the headlights of two cars coming out of the Kennedys' driveway. The cars stopped right in front of the Rumfoord Cottage. Whoever was in them seemed to be giving the place a good looking-over.

The Commodore went to that side of the veranda, to find out what was going on. And I heard the voice of the President of the United States coming from the car in front.

"Commodore Rumfoord," said the President, "may I ask what is wrong with your Goldwater sign?"

"Nothing, Mr. President," said the Commodore respectfully.

"Then why isn't it on?" asked the President.

"I just didn't feel like turning it on tonight, sir," said the Commodore.

"I have Mr. Khrushchev's son-in-law with me," said the President, "He would very much enjoy seeing it."

"Yes, sir," said the Commodore. He was right by the switch. He turned it on. The whole neighborhood was bathed in flashing light.

"Thank you," said the President. "And leave it on, would you please?"

"Sir?" said the Commodore.

The cars started to pull away slowly. "That way," said the President, "I can find my way home."

Herman Melville

....

Nantucket

NANTUCKET! TAKE OUT your map and look at it. See what a real corner of the world it occupies; how it stands there, away off shore, more lonely than the Eddystone lighthouse. Look at it—a mere hillock, and elbow of sand; all beach, without a background. There is more sand there than you would use in twenty years as a substitute for blotting paper. Some gamesome wights will tell you that they have to plant weeds there, they don't grow naturally; they import Canada thistles; that they have to send beyond seas for a spile to

---

Herman Melville had intended to write another whaling tale in the tradition of Typee and Omoo. He had "almost finished" Moby-Dick when he met Nathaniel Hawthorne and, under Hawthorne's guidance, completely revised the manuscript.

stop a leak in an oil cask; that pieces of wood in Nantucket are carried about like bits of the true cross in Rome; that people there plant toadstools before their houses, to get under the shade in summer time; that one blade of grass makes an oasis, three blades in a day's walk a prairie; that they wear quicksand shoes, something like Laplander snowshoes; that they are so shut up, belted about, every way inclosed, surrounded, and made an utter island of by the ocean, that to their very chairs and tables small clams will sometimes be found adhering, as to the backs of sea turtles. But these extravaganzas only show that Nantucket is no Illinois.

Look now at the wondrous traditional story of how this island was settled by the red-men. Thus goes the legend. In olden times an eagle swooped down upon the New England coast, and carried off an infant Indian in his talons. With loud lament the parents saw their child borne out of sight over the wide waters. They resolved to follow in the same direction. Setting out in their canoes, after a perilous passage they discovered the island, and there they found an empty ivory casket,—the poor little Indian's skeleton.

What wonder, then, that these Nantucketers, born on a beach, should take to the sea for a livelihood! They first caught crabs and quohogs in the sand; grown bolder, they waded out with nets for mackerel; more experienced, they pushed off in boats and captured cod;

and at last, launching a navy of great ships on the sea, explored this watery world; put an incessant belt of circumnavigations round it; peeped in at Behring's Straits; and in all seasons and all oceans declared everlasting war with the mightiest animated mass that has survived the flood; most monstrous and most mountainous! That Himmalehan, salt-sea Mastodon, clothed with such portentousness of unconscious power, that his very panics are more to be dreaded than his most fearless and malicious assaults!

And thus have these naked Nantucketers, these sea hermits, issuing from their ant-hill in the sea, overrun and conquered the watery world like so many Alexanders; parcelling out among them the Atlantic, Pacific, and Indian oceans, as the three pirate powers did Poland. Let America add Mexico to Texas, and pile Cuba upon Canada; let the English overswarm all India, and hang out their blazing banner from the sun; two thirds of this terraqueous globe are the Nantucketer's. For the sea is his; he owns it, as Emperors own empires; other seamen having but a right of way through it. Merchant ships are but extension bridges; armed ones but floating forts; even pirates and privateers, though following the sea as highwaymen the road, they but plunder other ships, other fragments of the land like themselves, without seeking to draw their living from the bottomless deep itself. The Nantucketer, he alone resides and riots on the sea; he alone, in Bible language, goes down to it in ships; to and fro ploughing it as his own special plantation. There is his home; there lies his business, which a Noah's flood would not interrupt, though it overwhelmed all the millions in China. He lives on the sea, as prairie cocks in the prairie; he hides among the waves, he climbs them as chamois hunters climb the Alps. For years he knows not the land; so that when he comes to it at last, it smells like another world, more strangely than the moon would to an Earthsman. With the landless gull, that at sunset folds her wings and is rocked to sleep between billows; so at nightfall, the Nantucketer, out of sight of land, furls his sail, and lays him to his rest, while under his very pillow rush herds of walruses and whales.

Edmund Wilson

···························

Going Out to the Traps

AUGUST 12, 1930. Beautiful night, with light marine blue of sky above sand dunes, with white cloud to the east shaped low and undulated like a sand dune, with the stars sprinkled close around its edges—almost (the stars) as informal and unnightlike as if they were some phenomenon of day—perfect calm night with full moon up.—Moonlit sand dunes: pure and bluish pale soft outlines.—In the town, all the houses, packed full with their large green-blinded windows in their compact white boxes, looked clear and fine in the bluish

---

Literary critic Edmund Wilson's reputation was established with the publication of his book of essays, Axel's Castle. Wilson was long an active force in the literary communities of New York, Provincetown and Wellfleet, his home for over 30 years. This is from his posthumous autobiography, The Thirties.

moonlight, with that New England dignity, one of the only things we have comparable in that line to Europe— a conversation, something in the nature of an argument, coming out of one of the only houses that were lighted.—We had taken along shredded-wheat biscuit and condensed milk and coffee, with orange-peel alky [local argot for alcohol] in it.

Everything was dark on the gray long pier, with its wooden apparatus overhead and its stink of fish—we sat on the end and had a drink—the moon was so thin, a bright disc placed lightly on the light night blue of the west, and toward Truro, the low gray-pink above the opaque blue of low clouds was reflected in the blue porcelain (a softer zinc) of the water, where the darker dories and rowboats lay parallel to the darker clouds— dark-faced shapeless figures on the wharf—they got down into a dory, five of them, from the other tine of the pier and rowed out toward the traps with regular heavy and funereal rhythm of oars, not saying a word.

We visited a series of four traps—the laborious pulling up of the nets: the butterfish, great flapping silver flakes, making a smacking crepitation of fireworks when they were thrown onto the floor of the boat—the squid would usually be the first to appear, streaming through the water in rusted streaks—they seemed so futile, so unpleasantly uncannily incomplete flimsy forms of life, with their round expressionless eyes, like eyes painted—a white iris with a black spot—on some naïve toy, their plumes like the ostrich feathers of some Renaissance woman of the court in an engraving by [Jacques] Callot, and their squirting method of propulsion, they couldn't even swim like fish—when pulled up, they would squirt their last squirt, trying to propel themselves away, then expire indistinguishably in a mixed bluish and amberish carpet of slime, when they would be sold by the basket as bait for trawlers.—Combined squeaking of squids and slapping of other fish, as baskets are emptied.—The first things we saw, however, were little sea crabs, clinging to the meshes of the net, which seemed, with their blue and pink, to match the dawn.—The mackerel, with their little clean-clipped tail like neat little efficient propellers: everything the squids were not—iridescent mother-of-pearl along the bellies and striped distinctly black and green along their blacks—a big goosefish: the old Portuguese fisherman held him up for us to see his great gullet with the limp slimy squids drooling out of it, brutally grasping him with his thumb and finger in the fish's dull eyes, then flung him overboard—dogfish with their mean smug sharks' mouths on the white underside and their ugly absurd sharks' eyes with a gray cat-pupil on a whitish lozenge of iris—when you held them up by the tail, they snapped up like springs and tried to bite you.—A few whiting and cod-headed hake—rather prettily mottled sand dabs.

It was cold perched on the roof of the little cabin, but as the full summer sun rose, we could feel its heat growing steady.—A gray warship of some kind farther out in the harbor.—The blue shirts and the dirty yellow oilcloth of the five fishermen matched the sky and the sea and the unseen presence of the sand.

When we returned, the tide was out, and the wharf spindled on the bent stems of its piles, green-slimed almost to the top—we walked into shore on the hard smelly slime of the harbor bottom.

Edna St. Vincent Millay

Memory of Cape Cod

THE WIND IN the ash tree sounds like surf on
   the shore at Truro.
I will shut my eyes.
Hush. Be still with your silly pleading sheep on
   Shilling Stone Hill.
They said, come along.
They said, leave your pebbles on the sand
   and come along.
It's long after sunset.

Edna St. Vincent Millay gained literary notoriety at an early age with the
publication of Renascence. Millay had many connections to the Cape,
including her affiliation with the Provincetown Players, for whom she wrote
a number of plays.

The mosquitoes will be thick in the pine
   woods along by Long Neck.
The winds died down. They said, leave your
   pebbles on the sand and your shells too
   and come along.
We'll find you another beach like the beach
   at Truro.
Let me listen to the wind in the ash.
It sounds like surf on the shore.

Paul Theroux

....

Summertime on the Cape

WHEN I'VE HAD it up to here with people telling me that
what *The Guardian* needs is a good comparability study and
that, in flood, south Dorset is no worse than Chittagong, and
the petrol price is finally bottoming-out, and the Common
Market isn't as boring as Canada, and that all you need to
appear on television is a speech impediment, and that the
aristocrat who disemboweled that schoolgirl (his plea: "But
she had the body of a nine-year-old!") ought to have his Red
Rover pass endorsed, and wittering on about some gloomy
comedian's coronary, and shop assistants replying, "If you

---

*Because he considers traveling a creative process, Paul Theroux is equally at home
in the realms of fiction and travel writing. Born in Massachusetts, Theroux now
divides his time between England and the Cape.*

don't see it, we don't have it" to every question, including the way to the toilet, and that licensing hours have
nothing to do with the fact that most publicans are
drunk by 2.30, and that the Royal Family are overworked
and underpaid, and that Park Lane is like the Gaza Strip,
and dogturds are preferable to cyclists in public parks,
and beginning with every sentence, "You Yanks—" and
saying that funny old England is changeless, then I figure
it's high time I took myself away on a good vacation.

The point is that England is not changeless, and I
sometimes think it is no place for children. Though I
suppose if children grow up among the geriatric, the
frantic and the scheming they will end up knowing a
thing or two about survival, even if they do sing the
wrong words to "My Country 'Tis of Thee."

Most people go away for a vacation; I go home.
And I consider myself lucky that I don't have to live at
home, that I am for most of the year on this narrow
island. England has the strictness and estranging quality
of school. It is an old-fashioned place in which unpre-
dictable suffering is part of the process of enlightenment.
It keeps me hard at work because I find there is
absolutely nothing else to do in England but work. But
the summer is different. Ever since I was an ashen-faced
tot, I have regarded the summer as a three-month period
during which one swam, fished, read comic books, ate
junk food and harmlessly misbehaved. In Massachusetts

the sun comes out at the end of May and keeps shining until the first week in September. No one talks about the weather. There is no talk of weather in places that have a reliable climate. Once I recall staying in London in August. I spent nearly the whole month in Clapham on a roadside with a dozen crones in overcoats, waiting for a 49 bus.

There is no bore like a vacation bore, but I think it is worth mentioning why I happen to like this handle-shaped piece of geography, swinging from the crankcase of the Bay State. It is largely a return to childhood, to a setting I understand and one which I associate with optimism. Americans still believe that all problems have solutions and that one deserves to live happily and uncrowded; they believe in the sanctity of space and can be surprisingly generous. This is very soothing.

THE REALLY SERIOUS traveler is the healthy intrepid person who, with a free month at last, and some money, and badly in need of a break, picks himself up and goes home. The casual traveler is another species entirely. For him, the journey is a form of neurosis that provokes him to leave at a moment's notice—and he may never return. But the rest of us, for whom travel is the experience of There-and-Back, are capable of the longest journeys precisely because we have homes to return to. And when early summer drops its clammy hand on London, and the

English start crossing the Channel, and the idea of travel is on everyone's mind, I pack my bags and go back to Massachusetts.

"Pack my bags" is merely a metaphor for pulling myself together. I don't need to carry any bags home. I have a house on Cape Cod. My closets there have enough clothes in them; my tennis racket is there, my bathing suit, my other sneakers, my second-best razor, my pajamas. I am better equipped in East Sandwich than I am in London. I have an electric can-opener at my Cape Cod house, and a jeep, and a sailboat. I also have things like toothbrushes there. This allows me to go home empty-handed.

But traveling light like this can raise problems at Customs. Customs Officers in Boston often demand to know why I am entering the USA after a prolonged period abroad, carrying nothing but a book and my passport.

"Is this all you have?"

"Yes, sir."

If your entire luggage consists of one book, they take a great interest in the book. Last year it was Johnson's Dictionary, and the Customs Official actually began leafing through it, as if looking for clues to the meaning of my mission.

"You mean, this is *all you have?*"

"Yes, sir."

On one occasion, the officer said, "I think you'd better step over here and do some explaining." I was carrying an apple and a banana. I had no suitcase. He confiscated the apple, but let me keep the banana.

It is roughly an hour from Boston to Cape Cod, but once I have crossed the Sagamore Bridge everything is different. It is then that summer begins. A person who is tired of London is not necessarily tired of life; it might be that he just can't find a parking place, or is sick of being overcharged. But anyone who grows tired of Cape Cod needs his head examined, because for purely homely summer fun there is nowhere in the world that I know that can touch it.

Its geography is simple and explicit. It has the odd flung-out shape of a sandbar, with an excellent but boring canal at one end and at its furthest, wildest shore, Provincetown, the haunt of extroverts and practitioners of the half-arts such as soap-carving and sandal-making, where women with mustaches stare stonily at men with earrings. The Mid-Cape Highway, Route 6, runs through woods and salt marsh and dunes to Provincetown. To the right of this highway, and parallel, is Route 28, with a bar or a pizza parlor, or a fast-food joint, or a motel, every ten feet; to the left of the Mid-Cape Highway is Route 6A, "The King's Highway," with its roadside orchards and cranberry bogs, its antique shops, and pretty churches. The town of Hyannis is in the middle of all this. Hyannis is partly rural and partly honky-tonk; it has the airport, the seaport and the shopping mall, and most of the Cape's better restaurants. But Hyannis is the ugliest town on the Cape—it is hard to tell where it begins or ends, it is such a blight on the landscape—and it is one of ugliest in the world, though it may be the only place in the world where you can buy a potholder with the late President Kennedy's face printed on it. Cape Codders forgive Hyannis its gimcrack look, because Hyannis is so useful a place—it's where you rent things, buy things and get things fixed and go to the movies. You can't have movie theaters and charm, anymore than you can have condominiums and rusticity. "What a place for a condo!" is the developer's war cry. The Cape is under assault at this moment and there is no question in my mind but that in time the Cape will be nothing except mile after mile of tasteful cluster development, so tasteful you will want to scream and go away.

The motels along Route 6A are straight out of *Psycho*. *Cabins*, the signs say, and nearly always, *Vacancy*. Strange gray outhouse-looking buildings lay huddled in the pines, each one solemn and weather-beaten, as if concealing the victim of a late-night strangulation or Prom-goers who have just discovered the facts of life. It is my belief that the most comfortable restaurants may be found along Route 6A, the liveliest auctions, the best second-hand bookshops, golf courses, and the freshest fish. It is possible to spend the whole summer on Route 6A without ever leaving it—shopping at the supermarket in Sandwich, swimming on the northside beaches, eating and drinking at any one of a score of places. The best whale-watching boat on the Cape, the *Speedy VII* leaves from Barnstable Harbor. "I suppose you could call this non-directive whale-watching," the on-board naturalist says as he urges the pilot towards a quartet of leaping fin-backs, or the geyser-gasps of whale spouts in the distance, or the magnificent sight of a humpback whale thrashing its vast tail against the green Atlantic. The whale-watchers are almost always successful; only one trip in fifty fails to uncover at least one whale. Long ago, there were so many whales in Cape Cod Bay they were harpooned from the beach off Sandy Neck and at the mouth of Barnstable Harbor. They were dragged ashore and flensed and boiled in the dunes.

Cape Codders are not particularly hospitable people, and yet in spite of this resentment of outsiders, it is noticeable that most activities on the Cape are designed for the amusement of visitors. The golf courses and tennis clubs and fishing outfits invite the enthusiastic tourist to join them. From Memorial Day until Labor Day, the Cape is a hive of activity, and most things are possible: you can charter a boat or a plane, hire a Gatsby-like mansion, go windsurfing or eat great meals. In the fall and winter it is different. *Closed for Season* signs go up, and the streets and the road-shoulders are messier. There are no tourists around, so why should we pick up the litter? That seems to be the reasoning. Cape Codders know that they live off tourists and so, in an offhand way, they welcome them; the Cape Codder does not become really fearful until he meets someone who wants to take up residence. In general, the Cape Codder is an inbred and rather puritanical skinflint, with a twinkle in his eye. An old Barnstable man once tried to win an argument with my brother by howling, "My family's been here for four-hundred years!"

Never mind. The only thing that matters on the Cape is that you stay a while. A week is not enough, two weeks are adequate, three are excellent, a month is perfect. This isn't travel, remember; this is a vacation. After a week or so, it is possible to develop a routine. Working in the morning—I write until noon in my study, undisturbed; then lunch at the beach, a swim, a sail; a trip along the shore in my rowboat at sundown; then a shower, a drink and the evening meal; lobsters or spaghetti at home, or a trip to a nearby restaurant. On the Cape, every good restaurant makes its own clam chowder (or even better, scallop chowder). On the whole, it is plain cooking with sensational ingredients: what could be plainer than a starter of steamed clams, a main dish of boiled lobster with salad, and dessert of strawberries? It hardly qualifies as cooking, and yet it is a wonderful meal.

After dinner, it is part of our routine to play parlor games. We have a card game in which each side must cheat to win ("Kemps"), a coin game for eight players

("Up Jenkins"), a word game for ten ("The Parson's Cat") and the most elaborate game of all, called simply "Murder," which requires up to twenty people and—ideally—a fifteen-room house for proper play—younger contestants can get the collywobbles in this frightening game. If there is an auction on—there is an auction in practically every town in the Cape—it is worth going to. The Sandwich Auction and Robert Eldred in East Dennis are two of the best; inevitably, some of the items are junk, but as many are valuable, and some are treasures.

Morning is the best time for blueberry picking, and the best place is at the corner of route 6A and Willow Street in West Barnstable. On rainy days, most people take to their cars and drive slowly towards Provincetown, stopping at antique shops. This is a fairly dreary way of passing the time—dreary, because everyone else is doing it, and Cape traffic on a rainy day can be maddening. Much better, if the weather is foul, is to leave the Cape altogether for the Islands, where the sun might well be shining.

An ideal Island trip is the one to Martha's Vineyard. Boats leave from Hyannisport and Falmouth. The lazy or infirm can take a bus or taxi to Gay Head at the other side of the Vineyard; the energetic—but it doesn't take that much energy—ought to rent a bike and cycle to Edgartown, among the prettiest villages in New England. It is just a twenty-five cent ferry ride from here to Chapaquiddick, and about five miles across this wooded sandbar to the long beaches which are marvelously empty. Nantucket is distant; there is not much point making the long boat trip unless you spend a few days. But Martha's Vineyard is easily accessible, full of interest and beauty spots. What difference does it make that the locals are cantankerous rustics and sailors, and the summer people are howling snobs from New York?

As the summer passes, the odors of the Cape become more intense, the sting of salt marsh, the gamy smell of tomato vines, the mingled aromas of ripe grapes, cut grass, skunks and pines. Plovers begin to appear on the shore, feeding side by side with the Greater Yellowlegs and the Ruddy Turnstones. The snowy egrets are watchful on the tidal mudflats and by riverbanks. Cars with Florida license plates pass by, full to the windows with suitcases and clothes: they'll be back next year. Through the thinning foliage—the Gypsy Moths have left their mark—comes a train whistle of the Cape Cod and Hyannis Railroad winding along from Hyannis to Sandwich—this is the best glimpse of rural Cape Cod, and the train is run proudly and well. The beach plums have swollen, and the marsh grass is high and local stores are holding "Back-to-School" sales—and I get sad thinking that the summer is about to end.

At the end of the summer I find myself surrounded by some very strange objects. There is a pewter teapot that wasn't here in June, nor was the rifle, nor the rocking chair with geese carved on its arms. Nor the telescope, the miner's lamp, the ewer. It is all auction loot. Why did I buy that commode? Here is a bird's skull from the beach, some feathers and green glass sucked smooth as a stone by the tide. Around Labor Day I think: How lucky we are to know this place!

In July last year I bought a 1925 "Angelophone" wind-up phonograph at an auction for $50. This was a great bargain, and so were the records—a stack of them I bought for a few dollars. I have the original album of Oklahoma, Bing Crosby singing "Danny Boy" and "MacNamara's Band," Cab Calloway singing "Chattanooga Choo-choo" and the Andrews Sisters' version of "One Meat Ball." I also have Peggy Lee singing "Mañana." A fortune in memories for fifty bucks! But no, I don't have the one called "Old Cape Cod" and it's just as well, because I hate the song any-way. But I do have Gene Autry singing "Mexicali Rose." I wind up the machine and put it on, and notice a slight blush of autumn in the maples. A perfect summer is a dream of childhood: idleness, and ice cream, and heat. Everyone deserves summer pleasures, before the serious-ness of September.

The Cape in the summertime is a resting place for the imagination, a release from the confinement I feel in London, and a way of verifying that the excite-ment I felt during childhood summers was not illusion. I hope my children will have the same fond memories.

In the first week of September, there is a faint chill in the air, the foretaste of what is always a bitter winter of paralyzing snow; the surf is higher and whiter, and the hermit crabs swarm more boldly from the jetty. Yellow school buses appear on the roads where there were only dune buggies. We hose down the sailboat and put it in mothballs. Then the flight to London, to the clammy airport where, one September I heard a nasty porter snarl "You're not in America now, mate" to a mildly complaining tourist. I am reminded again that I am a refugee for the winter. I have always associated leaving the Cape with going back to school, and now that I think of it, it was probably my pleasant summers that made me hate school so much. As for the Cape: I'll come back to you some sunny day . . .

Acknowledgments

Introduction ©1995 by Alice Hoffman. All rights reserved.

"On Nauset Beach" by Adam Gopnik ©1988 The New Yorker. Reprinted by permission.

"Homesick" by Marge Piercy ©1973, 1976 by Marge Piercy and Middlemarsh, Inc. First appeared in New. Reprinted by permission of the Wallace Literary Agency, Inc.

Excerpt from Tough Guys Don't Dance by Norman Mailer ©1984 by Norman Mailer. Reprinted by permission of Random House, Inc.

"The Chaste Clarissa" from The Stories of John Cheever by John Cheever ©1978 by John Cheever. Reprinted by permission of Alfred A. Knopf, Inc.

"Mussels" from Twelve Moons by Mary Oliver ©1978 by Mary Oliver. First appeared in The Ohio Review. Reprinted by permission of Little, Brown and Company.

Excerpt from Resuscitation of a Hanged Man by Denis Johnson ©1991 by Denis Johnson. Reprinted by permission of Farrar, Straus & Giroux, Inc.

"Provincetown Diary" from Queer and Pleasant Danger by Louise Rafkin ©1992 by Louise Rafkin. Reprinted by permission of Cleis Press.

"Going Barefoot" from Hugging the Shore by John Updike ©1983 by John Updike. Reprinted by permission of Alfred A. Knopf, Inc.

"Arriving" by Philip Hamburger ©1995 by Philip Hamburger. Originally appeared in The New Yorker. Reprinted by permission.

"Mussel Hunter at Rock Harbor" from The Colossus and Other Poems by Sylvia Plath ©1958 by Sylvia Plath. Reprinted by permission of Alfred A. Knopf, Inc. Originally appeared in The New Yorker.

Excerpt from Ciro & Sal's Recipes by Alice Brock reprinted by permission of Alice May Brock and Ciro Cozzi.

206